THE BLUE TENT

RICHARD GWYN

PARTHIAN

Parthian, Cardigan SA43 1ED
www.parthianbooks.com
First published in 2019
© Richard Gwyn 2019
ISBN 978-1-912681-28-0
Editor: Susie Wild
Cover design by www.theundercard.co.uk
Typeset by Elaine Sharples
Printed and bound by 4edge Limited, UK
Published with the financial support of the Welsh Books Council
British Library Cataloguing in Publication Data
A cataloguing record for this book is available from the British Library.
Every attempt has been made to secure the permission of copyright
holders to reproduce images.

For Rose, in our tent of days

The mercurial water and alchemical quintessence are frequently described as being sky blue or azure. Paraclesus introduced the symbol of the sapphire from the Cabbala into alchemy, where it came to signify the arcane substance. Thomas Vaughan described the tincture as having the colour of 'a certain inexpressible *Azure* like the *Body* of *Heaven* in a *clear Day*'. He called the Stone 'an *azure Heaven*'. Elsewhere Vaughan wrote that the water of the sages was a *'deep Blew Tincture'*. To clothe in an azure shirt or garment means to make projection of the tincture on molten metal in order to convert it into silver or gold.

Lindy Abraham, *A Dictionary of Alchemical Imagery*.

In that single gigantic instant I saw millions of acts both delightful and awful; not one of them occupied the same point in space, without overlapping or transparency … The Aleph's diameter was probably little more than an inch, but all space was there, actual and undiminished … [I] saw the Aleph from every point and angle, and in the Aleph I saw the earth, and in the earth the Aleph and in the Aleph the earth.

J.L. Borges, 'The Aleph'.

I went daily to the Bibiothèque Nationale in the rue Richelieu, and usually remained in my place there until evening … losing myself in the small print of the footnotes to the works I was reading, in the books I found mentioned in those notes, then in the footnotes to those books in their own turn.

W.G. Sebald, *Austerlitz*.

Thou art a toylsom Mole, or less
      A moving mist
But life is, what none can express,
A quickness, which my God hath kist.

Henry Vaughan, *Silex Scintillans*.

1

I stand by the kitchen window, staring at a blue tent. It is pitched just beyond my garden fence, in Morgan's field. The tent is bothering me. It is too near the house, too close for comfort.

There is no sign of a car or any other vehicle in the field, nor in the drive that leads to my house. Whoever owns the tent must have arrived by foot. They are well off the beaten track.

I step out into pale sunshine and the air quivers with birdsong. To one side of the house lie steep woods, burgeoning green, and a buzzard hovers high above the trees, a speck in the pristine sky. I wander down the drive, to make sure no vehicle is parked on the verge, hidden by the hedgerow. Behind me, the house presents an imposing facade, the three upstairs windows forming a dark triptych, giving the impression of symmetry and substance.

Walking back into the garden, I come to a stop beside a tangle of rose bushes. From here I have an unobstructed view of the tent, huddled close to my house as if taking advantage of the shelter and security that such a solid building provides. What a foolish presumption. How can the occupant or occupants of the tent know that the house is not inhabited by a dangerous lunatic, some deranged rustic assassin? Why on earth do they imagine that they are safe? Lord knows, I have an axe.

If I were to pitch a tent in a field, while on a camping holiday, I would pick a spot further away from the only building in this part of the valley. Under the big oak in the middle of the field, perhaps, or beside the stream that runs alongside it, but not at the edge of someone's garden, practically under the eaves of their house. There is, after all, a lot of land out there, a great deal of green land. Why so close?

2

I am accustomed to solitude and since living here have become suspicious of any incursions from the outside world. I have few visitors, and have spent the winter – which, due to the recalcitrance of spring, stretched well into April – reading, writing and occasionally walking in the surrounding hills, or Black Mountains, as they are called. They are not black, of course; they acquired the name centuries ago on account of the perennial gloom into which the sky shrouds them when approached from the east, offering a promise of darkness and exclusion, a state or condition personified no doubt by the warlike Celts who once defended their muddy pile against the no less hostile Saxons and Normans. I suspect the owner, or owners of the tent have come the same way as the Normans, from the east, over Gospel Pass and down through Capel-y-Ffin.

Perhaps they lost their way in the dark, did not care to venture further into the field at night. Perhaps they pitched their tent here out of convenience, since it was not far from the road and therefore nearer to civilisation. Perhaps they were afraid that a bull or some other dangerous beast was loose in the field, or that they might otherwise incur the wrath of a splenetic farmer with their trespass. Or maybe they were simply tired, and set up their tent in the first convenient spot, before crawling into their sleeping bags. In which case, perhaps, I should let them sleep on. I am inclined, now that the sun is on my face, to treat them kindly.

The tent.

It is of a strong construction, with no manufacturer's label, nor any other marking to indicate its provenance. It is a two-person tent, and quite generous in width, set up with steel and wooden poles, rather than threaded onto a light aluminium frame in the modern style: to all appearances, therefore, a traditional, old-fashioned tent. But its colour shocks me. It is a deep blue: in fact, it seems to me, close up, that it is the bluest thing I have ever seen. It expresses blueness, as though rather than being a colour, blue were an idea or a thought: no, as if blue were an extreme, intense emotion.

I stare at the tent, trying to decipher what kind of fabric or dye could manifest such a distinct hue that it actually pains one to look at it. I turn away. My eyes have begun to water.

No sound comes from the tent but I can sense the presence of human life stirring within.

I have been bending over, my head turned side-on to the tent's entrance, as if awaiting some sign or message. I pull myself up, and look around, feeling my behaviour to be somehow unseemly.

A dog is in the drive, in the exact spot I was standing a minute ago, when I stopped to look back at the house. I have never seen this dog before. It watches me momentarily, then turns and leaves; I don't quite catch its colour as it runs away, a flecked grey or dull russet. The appearance of this dog adds to my unease.

The sun is well up; it must be warm inside the blue tent. Whoever is there will be getting sweaty and uncomfortable by now, unless they are too tired to notice. I reach down for the zipper, but just as I am about to yank it up I have second thoughts, or rather – how should I express this – I have a strong sense that this is the wrong course of action. I will leave the occupant or occupants of the tent in peace for now, give them the opportunity to show themselves, if they wish, but

4

will not act out the role of meddlesome neighbour, even if the notion of being neighbours seems far-fetched, I being an actual resident of the valley and they merely passing through. I turn and walk back to the house.

3

A few things about the house.

Llys Rhosyn dates back to the fourteenth century, but was rebuilt after the Napoleonic wars by one of my ancestors on what was left of the earlier structure. On the first floor are four bedrooms, two bathrooms, and another smaller room, barely larger than a cupboard, used for storing linen. Three small rooms in the loft provided sleeping quarters for the servants in the days when the house had staff. This attic space is no longer used. Indeed, only the master bedroom, with its wide view down the valley, is occupied now, although I very rarely sleep there, for reasons I will explain.

Downstairs, there is a large oak-beamed kitchen, a sprawling living room with various small closets and enclaves and – most notably – the library, which, apart from its eleven thousand books, accommodates an ancient carved fireplace, supposedly the centrepiece of the original building.

Clearly the house is much too large for single occupancy. Living alone here, I feel like a derelict nobleman awaiting his demise in grandiose isolation.

I cannot speak of the house without referring to its previous owner, my Aunt Megan, without whom there would be no story to tell, and with whose person the house is – to my mind, and the minds of the others who will inhabit this story – irrevocably associated.

Megan was my mother's older sister, and they were the daughters, by his third and final marriage, of my philandering war hero grandfather, Rhodri Parsifal Llewellyn and Myfanwy Mildred Vaughan, the latter being the only child of impoverished Welsh gentry to whom the house had belonged for centuries. My own mother died when I was six, and my father, a country doctor in Pembrokeshire, was married, within the year, to a woman who provided an almost annual supply of babies (and me with a rapid succession of little half-brothers and half-sisters). At seven, I was bundled off to boarding school in England, and Megan became something like a surrogate mother to me.

She had, by the standards of most women of her generation, led an unusually adventurous life. After completing her undergraduate studies in medicine at Oxford, she trained in psychiatry at the Maudsley and later in Zurich, where she worked under the renowned psychoanalyst, Marie-Louise von Franz: student, research assistant, colleague and collaborator of C.G. Jung. She then spent a number of years in Paris, practising as a psychiatrist, and sharing an apartment with an old friend from her student days, a Frenchwoman called Zoë, before returning to Llys Rhosyn in the late 1970s to look after her elderly mother, on whose death, shortly afterwards, she inherited the house. It was then that she started work at the Mid Wales Hospital or, as it was once known, *The Brecon and Radnor Joint Counties Lunatic Asylum* at Talgarth, over the hills to the west. She was appointed consultant psychiatrist, and stayed there during the last twenty years of the hospital's existence (it was closed on the eve of the new millennium). Considering her cosmopolitan past and the breadth of her interests and intellect this was, perhaps, a surprising choice of location, but she always maintained that once back in Wales, she hadn't wanted to leave Llys Rhosyn, from which the hospital at Talgarth was a short drive. However, she returned to France often, maintaining her friendship with Zoë, who, in the late 1980s, and well into her forties, was surprised by pregnancy following a fling with a jazz musician. And although Megan continued to travel widely when on leave – to South Asia, and to Mexico and Central America – and made frequent trips to the continent to stay with Zoë and her child, and for visits to rare book fairs and auctions (she was an inveterate collector), she always considered this house to be as fundamental to her as, in her own words, 'a second skin'.

Megan, who never married – leading to some idle conjecture about her sexual orientation – left me the house when she died, a year ago. Although our actual meetings were few in recent years, we had enjoyed a closeness that belied those long absences enforced by distance (I have lived abroad for the past decade) and it was clear that my aunt held an affection for me which she did not display to other members of our extended family.

In her will, then, she bequeathed me the property and all her possessions, down to the battered Mercedes Estate in the drive. What remained in various savings accounts and bonds – a substantial sum – was mine. The will placed one condition on my inheritance: that I was to keep the library intact and, if I were to have children, to ensure that the house and its library remained within the family. If, by contrast, I died without issue, the library was to be left to the Oxford College at which Megan had studied and, in mid-life, been a visiting Fellow.

The solicitor, a certain Brynmor Williams, who communicated the news of Megan's death to me – I was living in Mexico at the time, and received the call during an electrical storm, the handset crackling and hissing as he bellowed down the line in his fastidious south Powys English – emphasised the detail about the library, repeating himself not once, but twice, as though he had been instructed to ensure that I understood and agreed to this part of the contract before even considering myself the legal heir to my aunt's estate.

It didn't strike me as odd that Megan should be so concerned about the care of her library once she was dead. The collection of books was her passion, if not her obsession. There was, besides, much about Megan that was original or unconventional; I hesitate to say *eccentric* since this was the term always drawn upon by members of my family to describe her, sometimes fondly, sometimes with ire, depending on what particular social formula she had ignored or whom she had upset. I think she quite relished riling people with less natural wit than herself.

Needless to say, I accepted this condition. I have always loved this house; I know every nook within it and have wandered for countless hours through the woods and fields that surround it. During my years of travel overseas, this is the home which I always revisited in my dreams. Living here now is returning to a place always known. Besides, I had no house of my own, and very little money, so it was an easy decision. Moreover, the task of inheriting a library, especially one as well-stocked as my aunt's, appealed to me, for I am an ardent reader, something of which Megan was well aware, leaving a cryptic, handwritten on her desk – for me, as I imagined – and which I found shortly after moving in. It read like an instruction: *One book opens the other. Read many books and compare them throughout and then you get the meaning. By reading one book alone you cannot get it, you cannot otherwise decipher it.*

This advice, or directive, was to give me much cause for reflection over the year to come.

Megan had passed away – peacefully, as they always say – in the library, in her favourite armchair, by the embers of the fire, leaving clear instructions that she was to be cremated and

9

her ashes spilled eastward, from one of the nearby peaks, Lord Hereford's Knob (a considerate detail, bearing in mind the prevailing wind direction), a duty I subsequently carried out alongside a wheezing and disconsolate Mr Williams, who was required by the last will and testament to be in attendance at the ceremony: heaven knows for what indiscretion or perceived failing she was seeking posthumous satisfaction by insisting on the presence of the forlorn and guileless septuagenarian lawyer. Perhaps she thought the climb would finish him off. Perhaps he was an ex-lover. From what I have heard locally, and in contrast to my family's assumptions about her sexuality, she left more than one local man broken-hearted in her youth.

4

I know few people in these parts now, the local population having changed character since my childhood, the old indigenous families mostly gone, their houses bought by incomers. Some of the older residents of the valley remember me, however, from my visits as a child, when I holidayed here every summer. Morgan, for example, the farmer in whose field – at the *edge* of whose field – the blue tent is currently pitched: he remembers me.

When I arrived for my aunt's funeral last year he greeted me sadly, with a blast of whisky breath, and reached out a bony hand – as gnarled as the ancient hawthorn – as if, incongruously, to ruffle my hair, as one might a child's, before returning with a start to the present, his eyes glistening with unwept tears, a man of a race and generation not given to outbreaks of emotion, yet demonstrably moved at that moment by the passing of my aunt, a spinster – a term deceptive in its associations – perhaps remembering those summers long ago when I had been a childhood visitor to the house, or, retreating deeper along the rheumatoid and foggy corridors of things unrecoverable, to those yet more remote days when he was a farmer's lad and she a rebellious, wilful, young woman. He withdrew his hand slowly, reluctantly, so overwhelming was the memory and so inexorable the onset of age and the proximity of death, especially on this occasion, a funeral, refuting the passage of the years, the decades, realising that the man standing before him was himself – myself – approaching middle age and that such a tender gesture might be inappropriate, or at the least, misunderstood; and I do not believe he made that gesture consciously, rather that it had been a reflex response to seeing me, however much I too had changed, so lost was he for an instant in the vortex between the long ago and the indisputable present, and although to pat the head of a child would be acceptable, to pat the head of a child who has long since become a man would be regarded as the sign of an ailing mind.

I know few people, but am not lonely. Loneliness is not to be confused with being alone, with solitude sought out and cherished, even jealously guarded, just as I, at this moment, was protective of my little domain and for that reason suspicious of the uninvited appearance of the blue tent. Solitude could be a hard-won gift, and its disruption, or even the threat of its upset was, I realised, already taking shape, wiggling its way into my thoughts. Even the visit of the postman was an event: people who live isolated lives become like this, we get fractious about any disturbance in the predictable pattern of our days.

Although the pace of my life here is slow, my days are by no means idle.

I made my living, until last year, as a writer of articles and travel guides about places I had never visited (as well, to be fair, of a few that I had). It's very easy to do this, thanks to the Internet. I've given all that up now, apart from the occasional book review or travel piece, but I am never short of things to do, and in the library, where I spend the greater part of my days, there are many books to read. I must confess, however, that the more I look at the books that line the shelves, the more perplexed I become. I have this compulsion to find things out, to expand my understanding of the world, but at times it becomes difficult for me to identify what, precisely, those things are. Sometimes it is as if the pursuit of knowledge were a mirage, that every objective is forever in flight, throwing up behind it a string of false clues in the form of 'texts' that lead one further and further from any kind of satisfactory intellectual resolution. Perhaps literary study of this kind is, by definition, an unending exercise in digression, the pursuit of ever-multiplying footnotes. Could this have been the course of activity that Megan had been proposing for me with her cryptic note – 'One book opens the other?'

It goes without saying that none of the literary tasks that occupy me provides sufficient income to make a decent living – nothing near it – but with the money I received from my aunt's inheritance, I have more than enough to get by, and my needs are relatively simple.

From the start I have imposed on myself a schedule, and my workplace is the library. I try to maintain a routine for a very good reason: since moving to Llys Rhosyn I have begun to suffer from insomnia, and have discovered that unless I set myself a timetable of some kind, my days are likely to fall apart, and night and day form one seamless trajectory. At night I sleep little, or not at all, passing most of the hours of darkness curled up in an armchair in the library, or else stretched out on the sofa in the living room, attempting to read, or watching DVDs from Megan's collection. British films from the 1940s are my current favourite – as they were Megan's staple – and though occasionally drifting into semi-consciousness, I never manage to achieve deep, healing sleep. In consequence, during the day, I often slump at my desk, or else succumb to slumber in the very armchair in which my aunt expired, only to wake half an hour later; and although not refreshed, I go about my business, but without enthusiasm or energy, for sleeplessness drains a person in more than a purely physical sense.

Time spent alone moves at a different speed to time spent in the company of others. It shifts in jolts and spurts, and there are long lacunae in which the overwhelming patience of the natural world serves as a constant reminder of one's own insignificance, and whatever endeavour you have in mind, whatever tasks you set yourself, take place against the backdrop of an unyielding constancy, a reminder that despite, or because of, the changing of the seasons, the fall of leaves in autumn, the abundance of flora and excitation of birdlife in the spring, all is subject to repetition; a process of eternal return.

Seated at the big desk in the library I am able to look out over the landscape, which from this vantage point does not include the field or the tent but rather the woods that lie to the west of the house, these woods that I have known all my life, have walked in, spying on deer, collecting mushrooms in autumn and observing, when I am lucky, the nocturnal activities of badgers, or of a family of foxes, one in particular, the dog fox, who ventures out of the woods at sunset, crossing the dirt and gravel driveway where my car is parked, occasionally stopping to sniff the air before continuing on his missions of plunder and forage. I see the fox more frequently than I ever see Morgan, my neighbour.

I stare out of the big, latticed window at the woods of beech and alder that bank the hillside. The buzzard, my buzzard, is hovering at some distance from the highest trees when, with a flurry of wing-beat and a terrible shrieking, a posse of crows, a *murder* of crows falls upon it, flapping from the upper reaches of the woods, making their hateful sounds, harrying and feinting, closing in on him with their sharp beaks, swooping on the buzzard, which dives away, possibly injured, I cannot tell. How terrible, I think, to be set upon by crows, up there in the sky.

5

Around midday I make coffee, and drink it in the kitchen, while staring out of the window, before my impatience gets the better of me and I return outside. I climb over the low fence at the bottom of the garden. The sun is high above the upper reaches of the woods and a fresh breeze blows down the valley.

The tent still betrays no sign of human activity. I am emboldened by the strong coffee, proprietorial even. I call out a sort of greeting at the tent. Hullo, I say: anybody there? Then on a whim, I repeat the question in Welsh, my ancestral language, just in case. Since I rarely speak out loud in the confines of the house, my voice sounds utterly strange. There is no response, of course, but again, when I focus my gaze on the tent, close to, I am struck by the dazzle and intensity of its colour – its deep, electric, oceanic blue – and I feel something like a pain in the space behind my eyes. I squat by the opening and put my hand on the zipper, but this time I do not hesitate, I pull it sharply upward.

Inside is the usual camping paraphernalia: a sleeping bag spread diagonally across the groundsheet, a rucksack propped at the far end, some scattered hiking garments, strong boots, an empty plastic water-bottle, a torch. I don't want to look in the rucksack, I have seen enough. I am squatting uncomfortably on my haunches – there was no other way to enter the tent apart from crawling on all fours – when the entrance-flap drops behind me, and I succumb to what can only be described as a fainting-fit. Perhaps it is my prolonged sleeplessness, I don't know, I don't feel on edge or nervous, but one moment I am crouching, neither fully inside nor out, and the next I fall forward, into the middle of the tent, and at once I am drowning, submerged in a diaphanous blue, in complete and utter saturation of the colour blue. How, the question presents itself vaguely to my ebbing consciousness, can a colour so disorientate, cause me to fall into a swoon, as a Victorian writer might have described a lady's collapse at the dinner table? The archaic word seems apt: *swoon* fits perfectly the sensation of falling from a height, and then floating away, drifting inside this blue, blue space, this *zone*, buffeted by the blue waves of unbearable nostalgia for something that I have never known, *as in a dream*, with a quiet yet palpable drumming in my ears as the ocean sways beneath me, and I the sole object on its now churning surface, captive and hostage of the colour blue, pinned to the groundsheet with the tent walls flapping gently around me in the swelling breeze, drugged to this world of infinite azure.

I don't know how long I stay there before slowly regaining my senses, and then I shuffle backwards, arse-first from the tent, my face wet with tears, though I have no memory of crying. I wipe my eyes with my sleeve, half-expecting to see that I have wept blue tears, but thankfully no, just salt, just water, and I zip up the tent again, take some deep breaths and look around.

There is no one in sight. Yet I know I am being watched.

6

Rather than return directly to the house, I decide to take a walk. I follow a narrow path that runs parallel to the drive, then veers off and climbs through the woods overlooking the house on the west side. I walk quickly, to stretch my limbs and to banish the feeling of helplessness that overwhelmed me inside the tent. But there is something else, which takes a while to register: it is not only colder now, but darker, the woods dim in the fading light of early evening.

Shocked that I have been sleeping in a stranger's tent for several hours, I continue to walk briskly, as if trying to catch up with the accelerated passage of time. In the woods, swathes of bluebells carpet the ground and the smell of the soil is moist and pungent. Everything is breathing. The thick undergrowth, in particular, looks to be alive; small shoots press determinedly past the topsoil, surging through the weeds and mulch that adds its own damp aroma to the wild garlic scattered beneath the trees. The track I am following climbs steeply, and after ten minutes, just before the summit of the hill, a turning of the trail offers a panorama of the valley. It is a place where I often stop, to sit on a fallen tree-trunk. The house is almost directly below me.

I am about to take my customary seat on the trunk when I notice a figure walking down the drive towards the house. It is too distant for me to be certain at first, but it appears to be a young woman. She is dressed in blue jeans and a black top.

The stranger walks towards my car, and I can see now that she is carrying something in one hand; it looks like a bunch of flowers, a conjecture confirmed as she stops and bends at the edge of the drive to pick something from the ground in a place where daffodils flourished a couple of weeks ago, and still a few remain. Then she stands and looks around, turning her head towards the woods and, lifting her face, seems to be staring directly at me.

I doubt she can have seen me, hidden as I am by the trees; besides, the angle of elevation would make it difficult for her to discern any human shape, even one dressed, like myself, in a red shirt, but as she maintains her stare I feel a leaping in my chest, as though I have *been found out*, as though I were a fugitive who has been spied by his pursuer. We all possess some kind of instinct that inspires fear when watched from a distance by a stranger, buried deep within the mechanics of the reptilian brain, which reminds us that we were once the prey of other, ferocious creatures. But my panic rapidly gives way to indignation as she lowers her gaze and makes her way towards the back door. She doesn't hesitate, she walks straight to the door, which, as usual, is on the latch; perhaps she knocks but if so doesn't wait long for a response before she lets herself in.

I set off down through the woods at once, slipping and crashing through fern and bracken. It takes me the best part of two minutes to reach the drive, where I break into a run, not slowing until I reach the back door. I stop briefly to gather myself, before striding purposefully into the kitchen.

She sits by the table, watching me as I make my entry. A bunch of wild flowers sits in a vase in the middle of the table. She looks me over and smiles, not betraying any trace of nervousness. Meanwhile, my heart thumps and my legs are shaking. I am unaccustomed to such violent exertions. I lean against the sink to regain a semblance of self-control, and from there, of course, I can see it – the blue tent – framed in the middle of the window.

Shall I make us tea, she says, – or shall we do the introductions first?

Rather than wait for an answer, she gets up and reaches for two mugs from the cabinet (she evidently knows where things belong), inspects the tea-caddy, sniffs the contents, and scoops two spoonfuls into the pot. She must have put the kettle on to boil while I was coming down through the woods.

Sugar?

I gesture to the sideboard.

No, she says, I mean, do you take sugar?

I shake my head.

Milk?

I point to the fridge, although I know this is not what she means either, as she is already heading towards it. I am out of breath and have a stitch, but am trying, unsuccessfully, to hide my discomfort.

My, she says, you *are* out of shape, and smiles again, quite sweetly, stirring the contents of the teapot.

What – I begin, between deep breaths, still with one hand leaning on the sink – are you doing in my house? I could, within the law, shoot you. As an intruder.

She makes a tutting sound. How you exaggerate. That is not the law, she says, still stirring. Not in this country, anyhow. Besides, I'll bet you don't have a gun.

I don't answer this. Instead, I watch her unhurried movements as she prepares the tea. I notice she has long slender fingers and a small mole on the side of her neck. I appreciate the fingers, which look artful and expressive.

She hands me a mug of tea, and takes the other for herself.

Mind if I smoke?

This is the point at which I might be expected to bring an end to the interview, if such it is, but there is something that holds me back. My curiosity, perhaps. I am not, in any case, a committed anti-smoker, have been known to smoke myself; so I shrug, which she takes as assent.

Mind if we sit down? she asks.

Mind if?

She sits anyway, produces a pouch of rolling tobacco, papers and a matchbox, and nimbly tailors a cigarette. Again, I watch her fingers as they go about this business, smoothing the paper, carefully filling a furrow with straggly tobacco, rolling with one deft movement, inserting a filter and raising the thin cigarette to her lips for a lick, tongue poised. She strikes a match, lights up, inhales, blows out smoke, and picks away a strand of loose tobacco that has evaded the filter and adheres to her lower lip, flicking it to the floor. She sits back in her chair and hoists one sneaker-shod foot onto the other knee. Her jeans are a faded blue denim with several patches sewn on, small labours of love; paisley, velvet, a tiny square of red, a triangle of black.

In answer to your question, she says, eventually: you came into my home, I came into yours. What's the difference?

Your tent, I say. Not your house, your home.

Tent, house, whatever. My dwelling-place, my residence, temporary though it might be. You too are a temporary resident, if you think about it.

I have no idea what she means by this. Perhaps she is attempting to be profound.

Tell me, she says, her eyes bright: what happened to you inside the tent? I know that something happened. You were in there for an age. Don't pretend that nothing happened because it will be obvious you are lying.

Nothing much, I say.

See, she says. You're lying already. The one thing that doesn't happen when somebody goes into the tent is 'nothing much'. Not unless that person is an absolute cretin. So, please, what happened inside my tent?

I see no point in dragging this thing out.

I kind of collapsed, I say. I passed out. And then, yes, I must have slept. No idea how long for. I have trouble sleeping at night.

She takes a sip of tea, looks at me thoughtfully.

You were *so* collapsed when I looked in. Tell me, did it feel as though you were at sea, did it feel as if you were afloat in the ocean? Was everything very blue when you 'kind of collapsed'?

Something like that, I say, sighing.

She nods her head in an encouraging and sympathetic manner.

That's good? I ask.

Yes, that's good. Very blue is how it should be. Do we have anything to eat? I'm starving, do you mind?

I allow the 'we' to pass.

There's bread, I say, in the bread-bin, and I indicate the sideboard with the back of my hand. There's cheese in the fridge. Soup, which you can heat up. Help yourself. Not that you need any encouragement.

Thank you. I will make a sandwich.

She speaks in soft, clear tones, a mellifluous voice, and sometimes, as in that declarative 'I will make a sandwich', with a kind of engineered, suspect formality, as if she and I both know that conversation, or *this* conversation, at least, is a game, a froth on the substantial world. While she busies herself preparing her snack, I have the chance properly to regain my breath. She is right about one thing: I am in poor shape. I make a mental note to extend my daily walks now that the weather is improving, go deeper into the mountains, take a picnic, make a day of it once in a while.

21

She has prepared her sandwich but remains standing at the sideboard. She does not cut the sandwich in half, but lifts the whole round to her mouth and eats hungrily. When she has finished, she wipes a few crumbs from her lips with the back of her hand.

Did you make the bread? she says.

I did.

It's very good, she says.

This is already the longest face-to-face conversation I have taken part in for several months, since, in fact, my pilgrimage up Lord Hereford's Knob with the hapless Brynmor Williams. My conversational skills are in decline. But if my own words sound strange to me, so do hers.

Why don't you have a dog? she asks, slicing cheese.

I don't care for dogs, I say.

A dog would be company, she says.

I don't much care for company, I say.

She turns from her slicing and looks me in the eye.

Do you want me to leave?

No, I say, not yet. I want to find out why you are here.

That, she says, will involve a lengthy explanation.

I have time, as you see.

I gesture around me, meaning, I suppose, to include the kitchen, the house, who knows, the whole world, as though time, or its unsteady passing, were somehow integral to the physical space around me.

She fills a glass with water from the tap and stands by the sink, taking small sips.

The tent bothers you?

I sigh again, but do not reply at once.

Well? she asks, peering at me over her glass of water.

Where did you get your tent? It is most unusual.

She hesitates, but only for a moment.

22

Your Aunt Megan gave it to me, as a gift.

She clearly enjoys my surprise at this, and laughs out loud. Her delight is child-like, and I almost expect her to start clapping her hands. When her amusement has abated she puts the glass of water down on the sideboard and resumes her seat, but now with her elbows on the table, supporting her head in her hands, staring at me over the vase of cut flowers.

My name, she says, is Alice.

7

Your aunt was my teacher, she says (or I seem to remember her saying); and the mother I would have liked to have had, or perhaps – she ponders this – an older sister. (Very much older, I am thinking.) I know it's a terrible cliché, but meeting her changed my life. We happened into each other in one of those random encounters or coincidences Megan was so fond of, and from then on, until a year ago, when she died, we were in touch every week, by phone, by email … and I visited here, two or three times a year. I came to stay with her many times over the past ten years … but I didn't make it to the funeral, I can't abide funerals, all the trappings of death and departure, I can't stomach them … so I didn't come. Megan would have understood, I know that for sure. But I was with her a couple of weeks before she died, here at Llys Rhosyn … and although she was quite old I don't think Megan was really very ill. I think she just decided to die. And *pouf*, she died …

Pouf? I repeat, bewildered.

When I first met Megan, she continues, I was nineteen and in a bad way … my parents had just divorced … I was doing drugs, had dropped out of university after a year … I'd been in these parts over the summer with a bunch of people up on the mountain beyond the Priory – she means Llantony – some stupid kind of hippy commune. One day we had been taking magic mushrooms, I had no idea where I was, who I was, and all the lanes around here with the big hedges, never wide enough for two cars to pass, well she almost ran into me in that estate car of hers, and she stopped in the road and there I was, walking nowhere, completely off my face, so she sat me

24

in the car, drove me to the house and looked after me while I began to come down ... and that took quite a while because I had psilocybin poisoning and she had to call a doctor out. He, the doctor, was a friend of Megan's and he said I'd have to go to hospital and have my stomach pumped, vacuum my insides, and I was totally paranoid all this time, of course. Megan stayed with me in the hospital at Abergavenny, held my hand ... and afterwards she brought me back here and let me stay. I had to go and get my stuff from the community, at the farmhouse where they lived. Megan drove me there and I saw how she went about things, no nonsense ...

I knew of this community, or ones like it; sometimes in the lanes I have come across these New Age crusties in their beat-up vans, and have had to reverse to let them pass. Such groups of dopehead visionaries have been a fixture on the landscape of rural Wales for as long as I can remember.

I didn't have anywhere to go, Alice says ... my dad had gone to Australia with his new wife, Mum wasn't in any state to help herself, let alone me, so I came here and stayed two, three weeks, and Megan fed me soup, made with vegetables from her garden; she nursed me back to health, and she talked to me, asked me questions, talked about herself, about her life, and she read to me, she read the metaphysical poets, especially Henry Vaughan ... she was a very well-read person, as you know, but she was also thoroughly practical ... I needed someone like that in my life right then ...

Alice looks almost apologetic. Perhaps she is concerned about causing offence, in case she is portraying a closer relationship to Megan than I ever enjoyed. But I don't mind, I really don't. There's a magnetism about Alice that draws me in; reminds me, in fact, of Megan.

Alice and I talk into the night, as though her arrival at Llys Rhosyn were a long-awaited visit rather than a sudden and uninvited intrusion, and we talk about Megan, in the way that people do when they share memories of a person they both love, and I offer to heat up some soup, to which Alice replies that she is almost always hungry, especially when staying here at Llys Rhosyn, it must be the mountain air, and it occurs to me that she thinks of this place as home as much as I do. As we sit down to supper I am wondering whether to ask her if she wants to stay the night in the house as it is cold out by now, but then, I think, she might misconstrue the invitation. As it is, she starts yawning as soon as she has finished her soup, rises abruptly and takes herself off to her tent, calling out a goodnight as she closes the back door behind her.

When Alice has left, I go to the library and set a fire, kneeling on the sheepskin rug that lies before the hearth to spark the kindling, then add logs from a big wicker basket. The fireplace and its surround are of an impressive size, and there are elaborate carvings set into the stonework, depicting mythical creatures, the twin centrepieces being a man whose face is the sun and a lion who is either devouring or spewing out a second sun. Apart from the sun-man, the lion and the various creatures that adorn the uprights, there is a row of small friezes, set below the mantel, of a man and woman, or rather a king and queen (they both wear crowns), and they are naked, in various states of conjunction or copulation, sometimes sharing the same body (but with distinct heads) and sometimes sharing certain limbs but not others. They are encrusted with soot, and charred in places, but immaculate in design. The stone is well preserved. As a child I was fascinated by these carvings, and I inspect them again now. One in particular attracts my attention, of the couple lying on their tomb-like bed, while above them a cherub bursts through swirling cloud. I find a rag and brush away a quantity of soot, so as to reveal what I know lies there, a large

26

bird, possibly a crow or raven. Peering closely, I can also make out that the bird is looking down at another, identical bird, of which only the head is visible. The subtle indentation in the stone around the second bird's head suggests that its body is in water, that it is either drowning or else emerging from some kind of sea or swamp. The mason, or sculptor, had evidently gone to a lot of trouble to illustrate some symbolic point whose purpose remained a mystery to me.

The fire is blazing now; it spits and crackles, briskly consuming the dry wood. I select, almost at random, a leather-bound book from a pile on the desk, which happens to be John Dee's *Monas Hieroglyphica*, and settle into the armchair. The night stretches ahead with an awful implacability and I know that I will not sleep, that I will shift restlessly from my place here to the sofa in the living room, that I will go through my usual routine of trying to write a little, that I will give up in frustration and start watching a late night film on television or else a DVD from Megan's collection (perhaps *Brief Encounter*, again, but no …) and that I will drift off for a few minutes now and then, but never much longer, and I will shuffle in and out of the kitchen making tea, and in fact I do all these things, as I do every night, and in the end I watch Hitchcock's *Rebecca*, and I hadn't noticed before, but do this time – perhaps following Alice's questioning of me earlier that evening – that there is a dog in the film, a spaniel of some kind, called Jasper – a preposterous name for a dog. What a pain it must be to have a dog like that, which keeps running off, and which needs such close tending. It would drive one mad. And when I get up to make tea, for the third time that night, and am standing by the kitchen window waiting for the kettle to boil, I look at the tent, its colour muted in the moonlight, the blue tent that my Aunt Megan sewed with her long, slender fingers, and her slender-fingered protégée lying within.

8

Shortly after daybreak I drop off to sleep in Megan's favourite and final resting place. By the time I struggle into wakefulness it is mid-morning and Alice is kneeling by the fire alongside me, an iron poker in one hand, smoke swirling thickly in the fireplace. My first thought on seeing her is that she is going to smash my brains in with the poker. I have a fleeting vision of her setting about the deed with unrestrained ferocity, and I sit up with a start. But no, she has made tea, and hands me a cup and saucer, in Royal Worcester china.

I would not, in the normal run of things, have used this tea set, certainly not while living here on my own, and I am almost affronted by Alice's decision to bring it out from the Welsh dresser in the kitchen. But, even in this moment of mild outrage, I realise that, paradoxically, I approve, and I think: Megan would want us to use the best china. Of course she would. She always liked attention to the detail of things.

Alice is dressed in the same patched jeans as yesterday, and wears a large and tattered grey pullover.

I knocked, she says, but there was no answer, so I let myself in. I hope you don't mind. Do you always sleep here?

No, I say, rubbing my eyes and sitting forward to sip my tea. I sleep, when I can, in a variety of locations about the house. Wherever I happen to be.

Like a cat, she says, wherever you find a perch? But as she speaks, she is studying the carvings in the stone fireplace.

She turns and re-arranges herself on the rug so that she now sits cross-legged, facing me. The sleeves of her oversized pullover cover her hands like mittens and she clutches the

28

cup between them. Her auburn hair is dishevelled, loose ringlets brushing the bare skin where the pullover strays down over her shoulder.

Hey, she says, as though the idea has just occurred to her, how about we take a trip today? A mystery tour. I choose the place, you drive.

I surprise myself by agreeing.

We climb into the old Mercedes Estate, which in spite of its change of ownership still exudes the personality of my aunt: old-style breeding, and a benign, no-nonsense reliability. It chugs along the country lanes with a reassuring purr, which, given its age and lack of tending, is impressive. It is another fine day. Alice sits by my side in the front. She has taken off her shoes and is resting one bare foot on top of the dashboard in a pose of relaxed – but possibly studied – abandon. I let down my window and the scent of mown grass and hedgerow spills into the car.

Following Alice's instructions (she has yet to divulge where we are going) we pass the village of Cwmyoy, the hill behind it supposedly rent asunder by an earthquake on the day of Christ's crucifixion, then on towards Llanbedr along a slightly broader lane, its borders bright with purple and yellow flowers.

At Crickhowell we join the main road, and follow the river valley, past Bwlch, where the country opens out, with undulating hills crested by plantations of Norwegian pine foregrounding vistas of the Beacons and conferring on the native landscape the incongruous effect of a hastily-added coniferous tiara. As we descend a long sweep of embankment, Alice points out the little church, which lies just off the road to the right. Wooded hillocks punctuate the terrain, and close by flows the Usk, its water reflecting the midday sun.

I park in the lay-by just beyond the church and we climb the path towards the graveyard. A faded yellow placard advertises the final resting-place of the parish's most famous son, Henry Vaughan, who called himself The Silurist (after the Silurian tribe that occupied the area during the Roman era), with quotations from his poetic works: it also informs us that the whereabouts of the remains of his twin brother, Thomas, the one-time pastor, are not known.

They say Thomas was sacked from his job here, says Alice, for drunkenness and immorality, but that was a common Roundhead accusation against priests whose sympathies lay with the king. Thomas may have lost his parish because he was a royalist, or else because he was an alchemist, or on both counts. But I'm sure you know all this, being descended from the Vaughans yourself. In case you're wondering how I got into it, she adds, it's because of your aunt reading Henry's poetry to me when I was convalescing at Llys Rhosyn. She convinced me to go back to Cardiff and finish my degree. I wrote my dissertation on Henry Vaughan.

I wondered how much more of the family story Alice knew. About Thomas, specifically. Although he was one of the three or four most important alchemists of his day, information about him was sparse. He published a number of texts or treatises in English in the 1650s under the name of Eugenius Philalethes. Apart from his brief tenure of the parish of Llansantffraed, he is known to have lived in both Oxford and London, finally quitting the capital during the Plague year, 1665, and settling in Albury, near Oxford, where he met his death by inhaling mercury, or else – according to a different account – in an explosion caused while experimenting with heated mercury. A dangerous business either way, sniffing or cooking mercury.

In 1651, he had married a woman about whom nothing is known, except that her first name was Rebecca, but she died seven years later, causing Thomas terrible grief. The marriage had, as far as records tell, been childless. Vaughan is supposed to have been buried on March 1st 1665 at the parish church of Albury, but if this is so, no record remains. The registers at the parish hold no trace of him, and his brother, Henry, records in a letter to one John Aubrey that Thomas died 'upon an employment for His Majesty'. So, some mystery was evidently attached to the circumstances of both his death and burial; and, to compound the mystery, two years after his alleged death, there appeared in Amsterdam a treatise in Latin called *Introitus Apertus Ad Occlusum Regius Palatium*, accredited to Eiraneus Philalethes. However, scholars are generally agreed that Vaughan was not the author of this tract, on the dubious grounds that he had not previously published in Latin (though he was, of course, quite capable of writing it), and the rather more plausible grounds that he was, by all accounts, even if unproven, already dead.

Family legend, however, is that Thomas faked his own death – no doubt due to some fall-out from that 'employment for His Majesty' – and secretly retired to a cottage in an obscure Welsh valley, where, among other things, he had a beautiful and ornate fireplace carved, before dying peacefully of old age.

Bluebells grow in clusters around the peripheries of the graveyard and the encircling hedgerow blossoms with small white buds. I stop to examine some of the more extravagant gravestones as we pass by the church. The first to catch my eye is the statue of a robed and girdled angel, a star on her crown, holding in one outstretched hand the flower she has just plucked from the ground, an image elaborated upon by the words chiselled into the stone beneath her: 'It was an angel visited the green earth and took the flower away'. The flower was a little boy named Awbery, who had died on the

14th of January, 1905. On the plinth below the statue and its inscription, barely legible beneath a century of moss and damp, are the words: 'Good Night Darling, Not Good Bye'. Over a century on, the gravestone invokes an Edwardian world populated by characters from *Peter Pan*. Alice kneels to read the inscription. I cannot tell from her face what she thinks of all this.

In the porch of the church a note informs visitors that a key is available from the warden in the pink house to the side of the churchyard. I can see no pink house from where I am standing, and in any case feel no desire to go and ask to be let inside. The head of a hideously moustachioed man wearing a Norman helmet protrudes from the wall by the door presaging further Gothic aberrations within. Instead we amble through the long grass, sprouting dandelions and elder, towards the churchyard's celebrity grave, which lies beneath an ancient yew. Henry Vaughan obviously wanted posterity to know of his extreme humility, for his moss-stained epitaph reads SERVUS INUTILIS: PECCATOR MAXIMUS HIC IACEO. Here lies a useless servant and very great sinner. Three curiously bewigged moon-faces illustrate the slab, to what purpose I cannot guess. At the foot of the tomb, looking down over the churchyard towards the Usk, where sheep nibble the grass in a scene of perfect rural tranquillity, stands a brand new bench. I sit on it, while Alice studies the wall that supports the more antique, fallen headstones from around the graveyard. She stops in front of one and gestures to me that I should come and look as well.

I peer at the weathered headstone lamenting the loss of Ann, wife of Thomas Thomas of this parish, who died on the 4th of November, 1857, aged forty-five years. Below was inscribed *Gwyliwch, gan hyny, am na wyddoch pa awr daw eich ARGLWYDD*. I translate, at Alice's request: 'Watch, therefore, because you do not know at what hour your LORD will come'.

I do not know at what hour my Lord will come, Alice repeats, half-statement, half-question, and she seems, for a moment, to be lost, dazzled by the dire sentiment captured in those words. Not far away, with a keen sense of occasion, someone starts operating a chain saw, and its fearful buzzing tears in on the peace of the graveyard. Alice puts her fingers in her ears, again reminding me of a child. If I cannot hear it, it does not exist.

We leave the graveyard and head down towards the river. Woolly white clouds scud above the sheep-dotted hills, suggesting picture-book symmetry. A woman walker approaches: sturdy shoes, riding breeches, sensible blonde hair. A shaggy black and white dog gambols at hectic pace beside her, veering away in a wide arc, black snout hoovering earthward, tail rotating so wildly its hind quarters seem to be about to detach from the body. A creature delirious with life. The woman greets us with an upward jerk of her patrician jaw, and a cursory 'morning', as though the time of day were hers, and she were bestowing a portion of it on us. I return her greeting; Alice scowls and kicks a loose divot.

On our way back I decide to buy some meat, and we stop off at the butcher's in Crickhowell to pick up some lamb. I realise, as I pay, that Alice and I have already moved into a sort of assumed domesticity. I have taken it for granted that we will eat together this evening.

Halfway back to the house, where the road narrows after Llanbedr, the skies open with tropical fervour. Lightning dances on the ridges of the mountains and thunder shakes through the car, making the doors rattle. With my wipers on double speed the windscreen becomes unintelligible, a streaming globular chart that dissolves with each swish of rubber, only to reassemble chaotically in the half-second between. Straining forward in poor visibility, I flick on the headlamps.

I catch sight of the animal only very briefly, its eyes freeze-framed for just the fraction of a second necessary to make a vital difference. I slam on the brakes, causing the car to skid noisily, but harmlessly, into the bank. Alice is out of the car already, and by the time I have struggled across the passenger seat and into the lane she is kneeling, cradling the limp and rain-soaked body of a young sheepdog. I look around. Although it is not possible to see far beyond the hedgerows, I know this stretch of road well. There are no houses nearby and the nearest farm is half a mile up a dirt track. The dog lies in Alice's arms, its body pumping. I recognise it as the dog I saw in the drive the day before.

Alice looks up at me, wet hair in her eyes, the long pullover making her look as bedraggled as the creature cwtshed against her chest, and she says: I'm bringing it home.

Not 'back to the house', or 'back to Llys Rhosyn'. Home.

She steps towards the car. I squeeze in across the passenger seat ahead of her – the car is halfway into the hedge on the driver's side – and wait for Alice to settle herself again on the front seat.

You're going to be all right, Alice tells the dog. I'm going to take you somewhere warm and dry and we'll get you fixed up. She looks up at me defiantly, although I have said nothing to indicate that I don't want her bringing the poor creature back with us. But I have already decided that it cannot stay.

The dog is a half-grown border collie, with a dappled grey and white coat and startling eyes, one blue and the other brown. (Like David Bowie, Alice later claims.) It makes a lot of noise to start with, but by the time we have turned up the gravel drive of Llys Rhosyn it has quietened, and seems content in Alice's arms. We ascertain that there is no bleeding, but one of the back legs might be broken. I phone a vet from the landline as soon as we get into the house (mobile coverage is non-existent in these parts), and am told that the surgery stays open until seven that evening, so we get back into the car and drive to Abergavenny, half an hour away. The rain has eased to a slow drizzle and the sun is already breaking through a fissure in the blanket of cloud. By the time we reach the village of Llanvihangel Crucorney, a rainbow arches across the coppery storm-clouds between the mountains of the Skirrid and the Blorenge.

History repeating itself, says Alice, as she strokes the dog's head. Funny, isn't it? What shall we call him?

If Alice is to be believed, we have hit the animal along the very stretch of road on which my Aunt Megan almost ran her down a decade earlier. I have to admit this is a convenient coincidence, although unfortunate for the dog, an unsuspecting pawn in the fabrication, by Alice, of a patterned and cohesive universe.

The vet, a woman whose seriousness is compromised by large maroon spectacles, overwrought lime-green plastic earrings and hair streaked to match, attends to the dog while Alice and I look on. He plays up, is resistant to her attentions and nips her hand, so she gives him an injection – Ketamine, she explains, with a wink – and the dog yelps, then flops in a heap. The vet attaches a splint to his rear left leg, bandages it, and presents me with a bill and Alice with a small packet of pills that are to be crushed and administered to the animal's food. Outside, the sky has cleared, but evening is closing in.

That was the night Alice moved into the house. After the storm, and the prospect of more rain, it only seemed right to ask her to stay. I had the whole of Llys Rhosyn to myself, whereas she had only the blue tent. Whatever its special properties, I refused to believe that the tent was entirely weather-proof. So, while I set about cooking the lamb, Alice brought the few contents of her tent inside and took over one

35

of the spare bedrooms – the one she said she had used when visiting Megan. It made no difference to me which room she took. Once dinner was in the oven I ventured to the upstairs bathroom and found a cluster of unfamiliar, feminine accoutrements on the shelf by the bath-tub, which brought me an odd sense of comfort. I picked up a bottle of body lotion, unscrewed the top and smelled it. I went through the process again with the hand cream and a tiny bottle of perfume. I felt at once invigorated and displaced from my own centre, like a spy in my own home.

When we eventually sat down to eat, it was late. The storm had started up again briefly, but had passed over, leaving in its wake a light but persistent rain. The dog, still sleepy with the painkiller that the vet had administered before setting the leg, lay determinedly across the foot of his rescuer, his one cerulean and one hazel eye blinking in unison as he followed my movements around the meat while I carved.

I wonder which farm he's from, I said, hoping to remind Alice that we were not the dog's owners. I can't see why else he would be out on the road, miles from anywhere.

Unless someone abandoned him, she said, hopefully. In any case, I don't fancy trailing around asking all the farmers if they've lost a dog. They'd think I was a stupid city person.

I didn't know border collies could have blue eyes, I said, let alone eyes of a different colour. And that streaky grey coat is very unusual.

I checked it out already, replied Alice. While we were at the vet's. It's called Merle, the colouring. It's not uncommon, apparently. And the eye thing, it's called heterochromia …

So the dog with the startling eyes stayed – for now, at least – like its human counterpart, as though there had never been another possible outcome; as though there were a contract between the two of them, my strange guest and her familiar.

9

After supper, Alice having retired to bed with the drugged and pampered pup – which she has named Ketamine, following the vet's prescription, though I'm sure the name won't stick – I return to the library, light the fire and settle into my aunt's favourite armchair with A.E. Waite's *Works of Thomas Vaughan* (1888 edition). But the turbulent prose, combined with the arcane – not to say preposterous – subject matter, is more than my powers of concentration can endure, and within minutes I am, miraculously, asleep, and dreaming.

In the dream I am being stretchered into hospital by paramedics. There is a glaring purple mark or blemish, the size of a dessert spoon, on my inner thigh. It stings horribly, as though lacerating the flesh. Nurses bustle around me. I am given blue pyjamas and allocated a bed. The consultant, an elderly man, arrives, followed by eager acolytes, examines the mark on my thigh, and announces that I have an *Alice-head Derm*, a species of ailment that he, the consultant, has only once before encountered in his long career. The poor man is perplexed, but so am I. I know that I will have to show the mark to Aunt Megan, because she will know what it means. I find her at a fancy-dress party, a carnival of some kind, and I sway through the crowd of revellers towards her, carrying a tray laden with drinks. People keep knocking into me and I am afraid that I will drop the tray. It is vital that I get to Megan without spilling any of the drinks. Many of the party-goers have chosen to dress in military uniform from different historical periods, but I am still wearing my hospital pyjamas. When I finally reach my aunt, she is the Megan of my childhood, a woman of around forty, dressed elegantly in evening gown, and wearing a necklace with a striking pendant of red and gold. I lower my pyjama trousers and she drops on one knee beside me and inspects my thigh. 'You should take less salt in your diet,' she says, 'otherwise you'll get an Alice-head Derm.' She ignores my protestation that according to the doctor I *already have one*, and continues: 'You must never reveal what I am about to tell you, except to my child, and my closest friend, so that you are me, and I am you.' But she never tells me what she is about to reveal, because I wake up.

And there is something else, there is always something else, that elusive quality inherent to dreams which you can never quite recapture when you attempt to remember them, or make sense of them; the thing that constitutes the secret heart of the dream and which will always be beyond recall or the powers of description.

I am certain of those final words of Megan when I wake (with a start, as though I were expecting to be somewhere else, or even somebody else), but as the minutes recede and I sit in the warm glow of the fire, they seem less certain, less fixed, and I become unsure whether they are the exact words spoken to me by Megan in the dream. *You must never reveal what I am about to tell you except to my child, and my closest friend, so that you are me, and I am you.* I scribble them down straightaway, on a notepad that I keep on the desk. I pick up *The Works of Thomas Vaughan* and flick through the pages I was reading before falling asleep, in order to check that amidst the largely incomprehensible alchemical jargon and prophecy I have not unwittingly retained these lines and then attributed them to the dream character of Megan, but I can find nothing resembling them.

I check the time – it is 3.45 a.m. – and start leafing through the *Anima Magica Abscondita*, wondering whether I should move to the sofa in the living room for greater comfort, when the library door pushes open and Alice walks in, barefoot and wearing pyjamas (mercifully they are striped in grey and pink, rather than blue, like those in my dream). They are men's or boys' pyjamas, lending her an androgynous aspect and they suit her well.

I couldn't sleep, she says, settling down on the rug before the fire, almost at my feet. It is the same place she chose to sit that morning – or the previous morning – and again she folds her legs beneath her in a half-lotus. Alice wears a necklace hanging outside her chastely-buttoned pyjama shirt; a scarab beetle in gold, a ruby held between its front legs. It is the necklace from my dream.

Nor me, I say, although on this occasion the statement is not strictly accurate.

She sighs and picks up the poker, gently prods a slow-burning log. Orange sparks drift up the chimney.

That necklace, I say, you weren't wearing it before, were you?

Alice shakes her head.

It was Megan's, she says. I sometimes wear it at night. Or in the evening. But it's not a daytime piece of jewellery.

It takes me a minute to think that through. Alice caresses the pendant between her thumb and forefinger.

I was dreaming just now of Megan, I say, without thinking. She was at a fancy-dress do.

And?

I hesitate. Quite apart from the pet name the doctor had attributed to my unusual skin condition, some code of propriety prevents me from disclosing the contents of a dream to someone I have known for little more than a day. It seems almost indecent.

And nothing much. That is, I don't remember. She told me not to take so much salt on my food.

Hmm, says Alice. That's probably sound advice.

I laugh weakly. She knows there is something else, something more significant; I can feel it in the cadence of her words. Without intending it, my gaze shifts towards the desk, and the notepad where I have jotted down the words from the dream. Her eyes follow mine.

You can tell me, she says. But, of course, you don't have to …

It would serve no purpose to conceal what I have written. Besides, the offending name of my skin condition does not appear on the notepad.

Over there, I say, gesturing to the desk. She gets up from her cross-legged pose in a singular, fluent movement, takes the notepad from the desk, and plants herself on the well-upholstered arm of my chair. Her hair falls forward across her eyes, and as she sweeps it behind an ear, the back of her hand brushes softly against my face. The contact, though slight, sends a tremor through me.

She looks at the notepad and reads the sentence aloud.

Does this mean anything to you? she says.

I don't know. It seems familiar. As if it were something I had once read, but I've read so much here over the past year, it could be from almost anywhere …

Alice leans back on the arm of my chair and rocks back and forth, her eyes lifted to the ceiling. I get – or do I imagine it? – a whiff of patchouli, and a vague childhood vision of Megan flutters by me.

Nothing else from the dream? asks Alice, as she slides off the arm-rest and stands, facing me. You said it was fancy dress.

I am staring at Alice's necklace. Without thinking I reach

40

out and touch it, and I stand up in the process. My fingers graze the flannelette of her pyjama shirt as I lift the pendant, and briefly, almost imperceptibly, and without the least conscious intention on my part, the palm of my hand nudges against her breast, or rather, against the distension in the cloth made by the bud of her nipple. It is such a fleeting moment, and such minimal contact, but her proximity, the scent on her skin, and the inexplicable intensity of the moment together cause me to catch my breath, and for the second time in two minutes something inside of me shifts.

Alice takes a half-step back. I endure a moment's discomfort, feeling inept at my clumsy movement and incapable of reacting with the lightness appropriate to a genuine mistake. I'm sorry, I mutter. Alice's eyes are averted from me, as though studying a pattern on the parquet of the library floor. Then she steps forward, places a hand on my shoulder and looks at me, the notepad held tight against her chest, covering that part of her body which I have unwittingly grazed with my hand – the breast of course being an *intimate zone* of the body with which my fingers, unbidden, are not permitted contact, whereas my face, or more precisely my cheek, exposed at all times to the vicissitudes of weather and the eyes of the world, is not an intimate zone, which excuses her almost identical brushing of it with her fingers a few moments earlier, without even the most formulaic of apologies – and my own chest churns in a chaotic soup of anticipation or of desire as she kisses me lightly on the cheek, yes, the same cheek she had – no doubt about it now – intentionally brushed with her fingers only moments earlier, and, still clutching the notepad, *my* notepad, against her breast, Alice turns with a 'goodnight, again' and a parting smile, crosses the library, her feet silent on the polished wooden floor, her pyjamas with all the buttons neatly secured

41

and the collar upturned, out of the door and up the stairs to her bed. I hear the creak of floorboards as she traverses the landing to her room, adjacent to my own (in which I never sleep) and then the twanging of springs as she settles into the big, ancient bed.

10

Early the next day, sleepless and somewhat tetchy, I decide to visit a couple of the nearby farms, but not before leaving a note on the kitchen table for Alice: 'Have gone to see if any of the neighbours are missing a dog'.

I start with Morgan, as the nearest of these, and steer the old Mercedes up the winding, pot-holed track to his farm, which lies half a mile off the road just beyond the entrance to my own drive. I am greeted, as expected, by a posse of sheepdogs, five in number, of which one – with the same streaky grey colouring as the dog we hit – is particularly enthusiastic in its brand of fierce welcome. I am not put off, however, and stride purposefully past the dogs across the yard. One cannot afford to display fear on these occasions.

The view from the farmyard is spectacular. Looking down the valley, I can see Llys Rhosyn tucked beneath low wooded hills, the great ridge that forms the ancient border with England rising behind them. The stream that flows close to the house glints silver in the sunlight, and the whole vista conveys a sense of green serenity. Paradisal, no doubt. Not so the view across Morgan's yard, strewn with rusting cars and a plundered van, its bonnet flung open like the broken wing of some giant lepidopteran, and numerous green plastic crates, scattered at random around the muddy perimeter. The centre-piece of this study in neglect is the corpse of a tractor, half a century old, tyre-less and of indeterminate colour. I make for the barn, with my restless, canine escort, now less vocal. A few desperate chickens scatter on our approach.

Morgan is tinkering with another farm vehicle, the

successor to the tractor in the yard, his head and one arm plunged inside its entrails, his free hand clutching a spanner. I know to shout, as he is deaf as a post.

Good Morning, Mr Morgan, I bellow. I am wary, as Morgan is a drinker, and prone to violent mood swings.

He pokes his head up from the mess of metal and engine oil, wiping his hands along the sides of his dungarees. He must be eighty, and he moves with a slight limp, but he is lean and agile and has the eyes of a bird of prey, the beak to match. And he speaks in the old tongue.

S'mae 'achan, he begins, confirming, to my relief, that he is in a benign mood, or at least sober, and that he still thinks of me as a boy, and always will. Morgan is one of the few remaining indigenous hill farmers in this part of the world. Once relatively prosperous, he lost his herd of Herefords in the foot and mouth outbreak of 2001 – the same year in which his wife, Angharad, died of leukaemia. He never recovered from her loss, nor did he replace the cattle. He had taken to drinking and tirades against all forms of government, which necessarily involved a jaded attitude towards his neighbours over the ridge, whom he referred to, disparagingly, as *saeson*. Whereas most people hereabouts held an ambivalent sense of dual identity, the border zone having been, historically, pretty much anglicised, Morgan adhered to a more ancient, fundamentalist set of beliefs.

Come in boy, have some tea, I was about to make a *paned*, he says, somewhat to my surprise – or perhaps something a little stronger? It is eight o'clock in the morning, but Morgan does not adhere to any schedule, outside the routines of the farm.

I won't, but thanks, I begin. I can't stay. The reason I came … I hit a dog in the road last night, a sheepdog, grey and white, and wondered if it might be one of yours.

44

Morgan grunts. A half-grown thing? he asks, thick eyebrows raised. Grey and white, male? Good riddance to him. He's no use to me. An idle, wandering good-for-nothing, that one. *Mae'n dda i ddim.* You can always tell the ones that won't be trained. He chases the ducks and next he'll be chasing sheep and next I'll have to shoot him.

Morgan wasn't exactly soft on any of his dogs. That was the way of things, up here. Little room for sentiment. I wondered what had become of the rest of the litter, but knew better than to ask.

Don't you want him back then? I ask feebly. I was rather hoping you did …

Didn't you hear me, boy? I don't want him. If you want to keep the pup, I won't charge you for him. Wouldn't want to waste your money. Though, he adds wistfully, I might have got a hundred pound for him in town.

Now, that is something, Morgan being famously tight-fisted.

Really? Are you sure? (Though I have no idea why I am pressing this point, as I don't want a dog.)

Sure, boy. Think of it as a gift. In honour of your auntie.

When I return to Llys Rhosyn, Alice is in the kitchen. She has read my note and looks up hopefully as I come in.

You can keep the dog, I tell her. If you want.

I have no idea why I was so easily won over. No, that's not true: Alice wanted to keep the dog, and I wanted to please Alice. It was perfectly simple. The potential disagreement over the dog, which I had anticipated as a burgeoning irritation over the course of the night, and for which I had planned a lengthy speech, was lost without a struggle.

We decide to go on another outing. Indeed, I propose it, although Alice prompted me by suggesting over supper the previous evening that, while the good weather holds, 'it would be nice to do some more exploring'. It occurs to me that we should visit somewhere of special significance to my aunt: the Mid Wales Hospital at Talgarth, abandoned now, was once the largest psychiatric hospital in the region, and Megan's workplace for twenty years.

Back in the car, we head up to Capel-y-Ffin and over Gospel Pass towards Hay. A small herd of feral ponies near the summit eye us suspiciously, and Alice sings, her feet up on the dash once more. The dog lies curled on the floor. He can't believe his luck. She's given him more painkillers, so we haven't yet witnessed any of the errant behaviour Morgan warned me of, though there'll be time for that. Talgarth lies another fifteen minutes up the road from Hay.

We park the car and approach the site of the hospital with some trepidation, after contemplating a sign:

DANGEROUS BUILDINGS
KEEP OUT
UNSOUND WALLS
UNSAFE FLOORS
LOOSE SLATES
ASBESTOS FIBRES

**EVERYTHING OF VALUE
HAS BEEN STOLEN**
You will injure yourself if you try
to get over these gates or fences
CCTV CAMERAS ARE IN OPERATION

The main building is an imposing Edwardian structure, built at a time, following the 1890 Lunacy Act, when the mentally ill were beginning to be seen as more than merely an aberration, or embarrassment to humanity. The place contained a theatre, in an attempt to provide some creative outlet for its inmates, who were also encouraged in other pursuits, such as painting and sculpture. There was a bakery, a tailor, a printshop, and a home farm with extensive vegetable gardens: the place was designed to be self-sufficient. The location, too, was selected on therapeutic grounds, presenting a frontal view of the Black Mountains, so that those housed here might gaze gladly at the glories of nature.

The hospital has something of a reputation in these parts, having been adopted by aficionados of the paranormal as an ideal site for communing with the spirits of the dead – especially the insane dead. It had also been cited in the local press as the venue for satanic rituals, raves or – better still – a combination of these two activities. Despite its impressive location, it seems to me a gloomy, desolate place, but Alice claims to like it, without saying why. When I press her, she says it somehow feels familiar.

We walk around the hospital grounds, but do not wish to risk asbestos poisoning by exploring further, so continue up to the woods above the hospital, following a track to Pwll-y-wrach, the witches' pool. We do not venture far, as we have left the wounded dog in the car, and Alice worries that he may get lonely. I, on the other hand, am concerned that he may chew the leather upholstery. On our return, however, we find him fast asleep on the driver's seat.

Afterwards we drop in at a café on the site of an old mill in the village centre. The place is filled with a mix of hikers and locals. Busy for a Thursday, says the lady at the counter, smiling, as if she knows me, and assuming that I knew it was a Thursday. Perhaps she does know me. I'm terrible with faces and cannot keep track of the days of the week. We eat heartily and drink several cups of tea.

Driving back to Llys Rhosyn, I cannot decide whether the sensation of being with Alice is closer to that of new lovers, or of old friends. Since we are neither, and these are quite distinct relationships, I must be very confused. But I am, nevertheless, happy, in a vague and amorphous way, as we speed along the road, the verdant, undulating terrain a soothing backdrop in the soft light of evening.

11

Tired. So tired.

That night, after Alice has retired to bed, I spend several hours drifting through the library like a somnambulist, dipping into books, unthinkingly obeying the directive left for me by my aunt, that one book leads to another, immersing myself in the footnotes to one work, seeking out the book to which the footnote referred (which, remarkably, was almost always to be found within the library) only to be led elsewhere by a reference or a footnote in that second volume, and so on, before wandering out onto the patio and listening to the call of an especially persistent owl. I make tea and swallow a sleeping pill, the only reaction to which is an even greater detachment from any identifiable sense of self. There is a soft pattering of paws and the dog nudges the library door aside, limps in, and lays himself down on the sheepskin rug, offering a few salutary thumps of his tail on the parquet floor to acknowledge my presence. I continue working at the desk, scribbling notes and attempting to make sense of the inchoate mass of words before me.

After an hour or so the dog departs, and climbs the stairs again to be with his mistress, as though he had merely been checking up on me, on her instructions. I return to the patio and stretch out on a garden lounger. It is chilly but I am too tired to move. Then, from nearby, comes a gentle crunching sound, followed by a kind of strangled cough and a profuse expectoration. The crunching or chomping grows louder as the creature making the sound draws nearer. I cannot imagine what it is: a scrabbling, as though claws were being scraped across gravel or pebbles, then the crunching once again, and the spitting. I raise myself very slowly in the lounger and turn my head in the direction of the disturbance, to see a badger, immersed in his breakfast of snails, head down, muzzle hovering above the dirt, front paws positioning the catch before his snout, tongue darting out to snaffle up the delicacy, whereupon the crunching starts up once more.

My gaze shifts towards the swell of woods on the hillside facing me in the mist of dawn. It is here, eventually, that I drift off, my brain thick with fatigue and the merciless, circular, repetitive conjecture that sleeplessness promotes in its victims, waking an eternity later to the sound of movement, at the far end of the patio. A tartan blanket has been placed over me. Rising blearily from the lounger, I can see Alice pottering inside the greenhouse. I prepare coffee, and call to her through the back door. She arrives a few minutes later, a wicker basket in one hand. She seems flushed and excited. Her shadow follows, tail wagging.

I ask her what she has been up to.

Planting seeds, she says. She has found several unopened packets in the shed. Carrots, spinach, corn, radishes, beans, she says. All sorts. Of course, inside the greenhouse the tomato plants have all died. But outside, she adds, the weed is coming along nicely.

Weed? I ask.

Marijuana, says Alice, in a slow and exaggerated enunciation, while emptying the contents of a folded newspaper onto the kitchen table. Your aunt was quite an enthusiast. She grew loads of it. Or allowed it to grow, should I say. Oh, and if you're thinking of going anywhere today, I'll come with you. I want to get some courgette seeds.

Aunt Megan smoked *weed*? I ask, incredulous, fingering the

dry, rank debris of leaves and buds and stalks she has deposited on the table. It smells of cat's pee.

Sure, she says. A regular pixie pot-head. Didn't you know?

I confess that I did not. I have not had cause to go into the greenhouse since moving to Llys Rhosyn. It is something – like so many other things – that I have vaguely planned on sorting out, without much enthusiasm, at some point in the future. And I'm not sure I would have identified a cannabis plant from any other kind, given my general ignorance of horticulture.

So, I say, you're thinking of doing a bit of gardening? That would be handy. I'm more of a supermarket man myself.

Alice talks not only of populating the greenhouse, but of planting rows of runner beans, of potatoes and onions in the vegetable garden, and I do not question her motives, nor even regard it as evidence that she has decided to move in permanently. Besides, did I really mind if she did?

As for the weed, she says, you might like to try some. It could help you sleep, you know. And if you don't like smoking I'll make some cookies. Or tincture; you could have it in your tea. Or bedtime cocoa. She giggles.

Oh I used to smoke, I say, not wishing to appear entirely … what exactly – uncool, stuffy, antediluvian? But it's been a while.

I do not take Alice's suggestion seriously. While she is welcome to smoke herself silly on Aunt Megan's pot if she so intends, I am not enthused by the prospect of moronic lethargy that I associate with cannabis smoking, on top of my chronic insomnia. However, none of this discussion has any immediate consequence, as around midday, returning from a solitary walk in the woods, Alice declares that she is feeling unwell, and indeed she does look pale and drawn, as though coming down with something. She takes to her bed and when, in the course of the afternoon, I go up to visit her with some camomile tea, she is feverish, with an almost luminous sheen to her skin and dark circles below her eyes.

Alice seems suddenly small and vulnerable, lying in the middle of the large bed. She sits up and takes a sip of water, which brings on a coughing fit. The cough sounds dry and cold, while flecks of perspiration appear on her temples and upper lip. The sight of her looking so unwell, and the sound of her cough, make me feel unaccountably emotional, and I sit down on the bed beside her and place my hand around hers. I stay for a while, holding her hand, which is warm and sticky. She clutches my own hand tightly, raises it to her lips and kisses it, then lets it drop onto the sheet.

I offer to get her some analgesics from town, to treat the fever, as there is nothing in the house, along with some groceries and the seeds that Alice requested that morning.

Before I leave, I take her temperature. It is a hundred and two Fahrenheit.

Are you sure you don't want me to call a doctor? Megan used to swear by one of the doctors in Crickhowell, Dr. Homfray. He's a good sort. I've been to him myself. I had indeed, over the year, procured prescriptions for a range of sleeping pills, none of which worked, but which I consumed randomly in the hope of some kind of breakthrough, which, however, never occurred.

That really won't be necessary. Sorry, I'm a lousy patient. No fun at all. I just want to sleep. And I don't want to see any doctors.

I visit the supermarket in Abergavenny and buy a lot of fruit: apricots, strawberries and grapes, even a melon. I reckon that Alice probably likes melon. I also stop off at a nursery and buy some seeds, although I don't know anything about seeds, and the enthusiastic and thickly side-burned proprietor contrives to sell me a number of late-flowering perennials, as he thinks they will 'cheer me up at the end of summer'. Since I have no answer to that proposition, and since summer has barely begun – and who knows what one will be feeling a few months down the line – I let him have his way and return to the car laden down with trays of shrubs and pots with small plants in them, as well as a few packets of seeds. I imagine Alice might find a use for them when she is better. It's a fine evening again, and I pass no cars on the way home, which is just as well, as I slip into that dangerous semi-comatose state familiar to any sleep-deprived driver, and once I even drop off, albeit momentarily, to awaken with a gasp as the car swerves towards the side of the road. The hedges have been cut back along a section of the route, and the fresh clippings add to the scent of early summer, and when I turn into the drive I am awake and almost spry, and even forgetful of the singular detail that there is now a sick young woman in one of the upstairs rooms of my house.

As I near Llys Rhosyn, with the sun in my eyes, I slow down to negotiate the uneven surface of the drive. Around half way along, the track veers to the left and the house comes into view. Standing in front of it, dressed not in her pyjamas now, but an antique knee-length white shift, is Alice. I am taken by surprise and sound the horn in greeting, but she does not raise a hand to return the salutation, nor make any sign of recognition at all. She seems rooted to the spot, and there is something odd about her posture, about the way she is standing there, slouching as though propped up by invisible hands, or else suspended by strings, with her arms slightly raised at her sides, the palms outstretched in tremulous supplication. As I draw close, in her strange pose before the house, dressed in that ghostly white nightshirt in the close warmth of afternoon, she presents an alarming and incongruous sight. I park the car hurriedly on the verge.

Alice is rigid, perspiring and trembling, apparently oblivious to where she is or what she is doing. Her breathing comes erratically in sudden sharp intakes of breath and exhalation, as though she were gasping for air. The black rings beneath her eyes seem larger and more pronounced than at midday, and the eyes themselves are open; terrified, but unseeing.

12

I carry Alice indoors, lay her down on the sofa in the living room and cover her with a blanket. She is sweating and has begun twisting her head from side to side in irregular spasms. However, once she has settled, and I have arranged cushions beneath her head, her eyes, which have been staring, wild and unfocused, close abruptly, and she remains still, her mouth clenched shut and her body tense. It occurs to me she may need water, and I return to the kitchen for a jug. I watch the contours of her face as she appears to do battle with private phantoms, remote behind her flesh. She makes small twitching movements and sighs explode softly on her lips. Several times over she performs a complex little mime in which her eyebrows rise, her forehead furrows, the corners of her mouth droop, her head again twists from side to side a few times, she bites her lip and wrinkles her nose. She lifts a hand to scratch vigorously at her temple, then lets it drop, leaving a pink welt high on the cheek. She sucks in air and noisily blows out again. Whatever is going on in the watery depths of her soul is manifesting itself as a shadow play to which I am a silent spectator.

Her face, I think, is dancing.

I pour out half a cupful of water, lift the back of Alice's head with one hand, and hold the cup to her mouth with the other. She opens her eyes, looks momentarily confused, and then relaxes, slowly sipping the water, her gaze settling on me. When she has drunk enough, she lets out a little sigh and pushes the cup away. She smiles weakly, and says 'tired now'. She turns onto her side and within seconds is asleep.

I stay in the living room for a while, pulling up a chair close to the sofa, but Alice is out for the count, so I go into the library to find a book, thinking I will return and read by her side. I consider calling a doctor, but then remember Alice's aversion to the idea when I suggested it earlier. Besides, I reason, if she is now sleeping, the worst might be over. But on returning to Alice's bedside with a slim leather-bound book – Jean de La Fontaine's *The Pleasant Founteine of Knowledge* (1413) – I find (perhaps not surprisingly, given my choice of reading matter) that I cannot concentrate, and acknowledge with a yawn that although very tired, I am nonetheless too agitated to sleep. I calculate that I have slept a total of ten hours in the past four days and nights, that is, in the past ninety-six hours. Call it ten per cent. It should be between twenty-five and forty per cent, depending on one's metabolism. Folk wisdom agrees on eight hours, around thirty-three per cent. I have been managing less than a third of that. And not just for the past four days: for the past fourteen months, from the time, at least, that I moved into Llys Rhosyn. Perhaps I really should see a sleep specialist, as Dr. Homfray suggested on my last visit to his surgery in Crickhowell.

As I sit there, making futile calculations, attempting a personal mathematics of insomnia, with the ancient book of poems neglected on my lap, the image of Alice, desolate and trembling in front of the house, her arms outstretched as if in crucifixion, keeps returning to my mind's eye, and after a while I make my way to the kitchen, keen to occupy myself with something, anything to dispel this disturbing vision. I prepare a soup with all the vegetables I can find, thinking that when Alice wakes up she might appreciate simple and nutritious food. I put the soup on a low heat and step outside into the garden. A late afternoon breeze stirs the blossom on the cherry tree, and I wander over to the gate that leads to Morgan's field.

The blue tent is still there, of course. It shocks me that only three days have passed since Alice's arrival. But both she and the tent are now fixed on the landscape, external and interior. I count the days again. I feel confused. Time is not moving at the right pace. If yesterday was Thursday, as the lady in the tea shop informed me, it must have been on Tuesday evening that Alice had walked, unannounced and imperious, into my kitchen. On Wednesday we visited Henry Vaughan's grave, and ran down the grey and white dog on our way home. That night Alice moved in and surprised me in the library in the small hours. Thursday, I paid a visit to Morgan and then we drove to Talgarth. Today, Friday, she has fallen ill. I have known her for seventy-two hours, and yet it already seems impossible that I have not known her always.

With no particular motive in mind, I move towards the tent, again drawn in by the intensity and almost hypnotic quality of its colour. I reach down for the zip and, crouching, peer inside. It is empty, as expected. I creep forward on all fours, attentive to any signs of the weirdness that had wrought such an effect on my previous visit; but rather than any sense of being at sea, I feel the onset of an immense fatigue. Recent events have excited me, breaking my routine and conjuring the remarkable presence of Alice, and I am not prepared for this sudden and complete exhaustion. The consoling azure light, fading to white, provokes a weariness that spreads through my limbs, too powerful to resist, and within seconds I am asleep.

13

When I wake, I have no idea where I am. I have been dreaming wild and terrifying dreams and I am sweating profusely. I think I see a figure, or figures, moving darkly outside the tent, but something, or rather some voice – who knows, perhaps the voice of the tent itself – informs me they are the last shadows of my dream escaping back into oblivion. I don't quite believe this disembodied voice, but neither do I question it, at least not straightaway, and there is a malignancy on the air, a sense of dread that has settled in the pit of my stomach. I scramble outside, remembering with a flutter of panic that I have left Alice lying on the sofa, alone.

Indoors, the house is dark and gloomy. I rush through to the living room. Although, rationally, there is little chance of Alice having come to any harm, I do not feel at that moment as though we are lodged within an entirely rational place. I avoid switching on the lamp for fear of waking her, and then I notice, in the half-light, that her eyes are open, and she is watching me.

Hullo, I say. Have you been awake for long?

No. Just woke up. I thought I was inside the tent. I had a very confusing dream. Her voice drifts into silence.

What am I doing down here? she asks, eventually.

Do you remember nothing?

Nothing much.

I tell her that I found her standing outside the house in an old nightshirt, that I brought her in here. I do not go into details about her odd behaviour and she doesn't ask questions. I surmise that it is not the first time she has suffered a fit of this kind. Her fever has subsided and she is no longer trembling. She reaches for the water jug.

Let me do that, I say, and pour her a cup. She drinks thirstily.

I'm starving, she says.

The smell of soup wafting in from the kitchen reminds me I had been cooking before going out to the garden and into the tent. Perhaps that is what woke her, the smell of food.

There's soup, I say. I'll bring you some if you want.

Thanks, but I'll get up first. I need a bath. Then maybe we can have some soup.

She edges off the sofa, and I extend an arm to help her stand. She leans awkwardly for a moment and then, facing me, puts both arms around my neck. Her breath is hot and gives off the pungent, slightly sour odour that fever brings.

Where did you go, Alice?

She pauses, resting her hand on my shoulder.

Somewhere not so good. I'll tell you about it, but not now. What I need now is to be *here*. She gestures emphatically around her, with both arms, in a manner that suggests my inclusion within the defined space; then, blanket draped over her shoulders, she sets off, barefoot, up the stairs to the bathroom.

My relief at seeing Alice in this improved – if still somewhat disoriented – state sets my mind at peace a little. I make myself busy in the kitchen, and am preparing a fruit salad to follow the soup, when I hear footsteps outside, crunching on the gravel. I cross to the back door, but whoever is outside gets there first, and hammers on it with three loud raps. Not a shy knock, I think.

Wary, and conscious that my house is not on the way to anywhere and does not, as a rule, attract visitors, I open the door a fraction, and peer out.

A man is standing there. He is unshaven, of middle years, with a tanned, lived-in face. He wears well-serviced hiking boots, dusty corduroy trousers, a check woollen shirt, and his countenance is one of cheerful dishevelment. His eyes betray an inquisitive intelligence, and when he speaks he confirms the impression – despite his apparent material poverty – of an easy worldliness, and I am not surprised that his voice is deep and sonorous, suggestive of a westerly Celtic provenance.

Could I trouble you for a bottle of water? he asks. I foolishly neglected to fill a second bottle, and now have none to cook with.

His question raises a host of subsidiary ones, but I do not wish to appear unfriendly, so I put my doubts on hold and take from him the empty plastic flagon that he is waving in my direction. I gesture to him to step inside, and he follows me over to the sink, where I set about filling his container.

Are you camping hereabouts? I ask, as I can think of nothing else to say.

Yes, he says. I hope you don't mind. I won't be any trouble. But I picked a spot quite close to your house, in the field.

That shouldn't be a problem, I say. The field actually belongs to my neighbour, a farmer by the name of Morgan, but he has no objection to campers. So long, I add in afterthought, as you don't have a dog. It's the lambing season, you see.

Morgan had very few sheep, and they would, in any case, be on the upper pastures by now, not down here in the valley, but there is no harm in saying.

No, I don't have a dog, the stranger says.

A man such as yourself, I say (following a train of thought from some half-remembered conversation) ought to have a dog.

I don't much care for dogs, he says.

60

A dog would be good company, I say.

I manage just fine, he says, exactly as I am.

I screw the top back on to his water container.

Where exactly have you pitched your tent? I ask. I had been outside not fifteen minutes before, and there had been no sign of any other campers. If, that is, I add, you *have* a tent.

Oh I have a tent, says the man. It's right at the end of your garden, in the field. I'll show you, if you like.

I follow him outside. It is a perfect late spring evening, the sun casting long shadows across the lawn. We start down the path, past the cherry tree, and before we get to the little gate, he stops, pointing across the low fence to where the blue tent stands.

There, he says, not without a hint of pride, that's my tent.

14

My first reaction was outrage. Did this tramp take me for an idiot? Was it not reasonable to assume that I might be familiar with the existence of a tent, pitched as it has been, these three days past, at the end of my garden? His face betrays nothing at all, until he notices my disbelieving expression, and he then adopts a mode of unctuous concern.

Is anything the matter? You seem troubled, sir. Is there a problem with me camping so close to your house?

So this was his tack: he was going to play the innocent victim of my presumed intolerance. He was going to address me as *sir*, despite his not inconsiderable seniority of age.

Not at all, I say, in answer, summoning a smile. You are quite welcome to camp here.

I keep up my benevolent rictus for longer than strictly necessary, until the muscles in my cheeks begin to ache. Wandering over to the tent, I pretend to inspect it for the first time.

That's a fine looking tent you have.

It does the job, he says. Keeps the rain off and that.

Had it for long?

As a matter of fact I have, he says. It was a gift from a dear friend, now sadly passed away.

Indeed? I say. A generous bequest. And, let me see, in this light it is hard to make out, but it is blue, is it not? A most striking blue, if I am not mistaken.

Aye, says the man. It is that. As blue as the midsummer sky.

Do you intend staying long? I ask.

What, tired of me already? He grins, in the fashion of a man accustomed to charming the susceptible.

Ha ha ha, not at all. As I said, the field belongs to my neighbour, Mister Morgan. If you wander over to the farmhouse of a morning, just over the next field there, and up the lane, you may have milk for breakfast, fresh from the cow.

I have made that up, of course. It was a long time since milk had ceased to be Morgan's beverage of choice. And if he walked over to Morgan's farm of a morning, and found the old bastard sober, it would be a miracle indeed if he escaped without the seat of his pants being ripped to shreds by one of Morgan's dogs.

Is that so? Well, it'll be like a friggin' Famous Five adventure for me here then, so it will.

There is something sinister in the way he says that.

Quite so, I reply, and, realising this is the moment at which I am probably expected to take my leave, whereupon the stranger would go about the business of cooking his meal – I can see he has a primus stove set up, a tin of beans, a sliced loaf, a flagon of cider, an enamel plate and mug – I swiftly settle on a course of action. I will expose this vagrant's ridiculous fantasy and have done with it, pointing out that the tent is not his, that he is not welcome, and that he must pack up at once, failing which I will call the police.

But just then I hear Alice's voice behind me, bright as birdsong. I turn around. She has washed her hair, and is wearing a summer dress and a cashmere cardigan, rather than her usual jeans, T-shirt and man's pullover. At her open neck she wears the scarab pendant. All signs of the mystery illness have vanished from her face. Her glossy auburn hair is brushed back, her cheeks are glowing and the black rings below her eyes have gone. She is wearing lipstick, a deep red that complements her hair colour. Her presence exudes a kind

63

of demure sophistication, which has been entirely absent until now. It is as though she has been transformed into a woman of style and accomplishment.

Is everything all right? Alice asks.

I am caught between astonishment at the change that has come over her, and irritation that she has appeared at all, disrupting my plan of action, which I was intending to carry out without involving her in a dispute that might turn ugly.

I see we have a visitor, she continues. Aren't you going to introduce us?

This completely throws me. I would have expected Alice to express alarm or anger at seeing this stranger make free with her tent, especially considering the emotional attachment I know it holds for her. But instead I struggle to say anything at all, mumble my apologies and confess that I do not know the stranger's name.

O'Hallaran, he says, and if he had been wearing a hat he would have doffed it. Charming evening, is it not?

I stand there, piggy in the middle, not knowing which way to turn. Alice seems oblivious to any wrongdoing on the part of this O'Hallaran with regard to the tent. Perhaps, despite her transformation from boho chic to *Vogue* model, she is still a bit funny in the head following her fever.

But Alice, I object, *your tent*.

She looks at me curiously and, I think, rather too tenderly, as if it were I who had been unwell – or suffered from some mental ailment – and not she.

This chap – I continue, quite unnecessarily – says it's his. He says he's just arrived. With *your tent*. I am becoming quite animated.

Oh now, that's impossible. He must have a blue tent also, she says, as though it were dim of me not to have reached this conclusion myself.

But it's the *same* tent, I insist, my frustration mounting. It's the same blue tent my Aunt Megan made for you, Alice, *the same fucking tent!*

I am pointing at it, my index finger quivering, my voice hoarse.

The same tent? She looks it over, summarily. Perhaps it is. I doubt it somehow. And anyway, does it matter? I do think you are getting a little over-excited. Why don't we go inside and have some of that soup you've been making? We could invite Mister O'Hallaran to share some with us, don't you think?

Before I have a chance to reply, the vagabond does so for me, expressing his acceptance of the offer, with a simpering gratitude: *most kind, much obliged … I will be along shortly.*

He makes me want to spit.

But Alice has taken my arm, again as though I, not she, were the invalid, and is beginning to lead me across the garden, back to the house. I stop after a few paces. O'Hallaran is behind us, rummaging in the tent.

Look, I say, speaking fast but keeping my voice low, I need to clear something up, otherwise I'll be worried that I'm going off my trolley. That blue tent, over there – *that* one – and again I point at it, as though there were a plurality of tents to choose amongst – is *your* tent. You arrived here with that tent on Monday night. You told me that my aunt made you the tent: she sewed it herself, with materials she had dyed blue, extremely blue. And now this O'Hallaran fellow emerges from the very same tent and claims it's his. And you say nothing to contradict him. First you say the tent is not the same one – it's impossible, you say – then you suggest that it might be the same but you cannot be sure. But neither way does it seem to matter much to you. What is going on?

Alice turns aside to make sure O'Hallaran is still out of

earshot and – with her hand on my arm – says: there are a few things I don't quite understand about the blue tent. This may be one of them. It sometimes … how should I put this … coughs up a few surprises. But on such occasions it's best just to go with the flow, do you see?

I don't see. I can't see and I don't want to see. But I start back to the house with her anyway.

15

O'Hallaran turns out to be a civil enough dinner guest; at least he is familiar with the use of cutlery, and I don't know whether it's due to Alice's benign influence, but the slight sense of menace I discerned in him earlier – when I teased him about early morning milk from Morgan's farm – does not re-surface during the course of the meal.

I am, more than anything else, impressed by Alice's marvellous recuperation. When I left her to take her bath she had seemed extremely fragile, and I imagined she would need several days to convalesce, but now she is refreshed, radiant even, and not remotely perturbed by the unexpected appearance of O'Hallaran.

I, on the contrary, am exceedingly perturbed. Put out and confounded. I suspect that O'Hallaran is a scoundrel, and that his intentions are of the worst kind. I decide to test him further.

How did you settle on this neck of the woods, I ask him, for a camping holiday?

Camping holiday? He repeats the words slowly, as though the very notion amused him. I am not on a camping holiday.

Really? I say. So this is a lifestyle choice? You are a gentleman of the road, a vagabond? I did not know there were still such things. I thought they had disappeared around the same time as black and white televisions and popcorn ceilings. I know about the urban homeless poor and have encountered them in droves around the planet. I am also familiar with the sight of so-called travellers in vans, New Age or otherwise, cluttering up our country lanes, but the solitary foot-slogging rural tramp? The wild rover, striding forth from the lyrics of a *Dubliners* song? You impress me, Mister O'Hallaran, with your fine sense of anachronism.

A glance from Alice suggests I have gone too far with this outburst.

I apologise, I say hastily. I am very tired and have forgotten my manners. I have lived abroad for many years, I add, though I have no idea how or why that should make any difference, nor why I have said it.

Is that so? says O'Hallaran, helping himself to a thick slab of my bread and buttering it generously. And where, he says, were you living, whilst *abroad*?

He enunciates the word as though it were a place of my own invention.

Oh, here and there, I reply. Burkina Faso, Sumatra, Belize. How about yourself? Is your vagabondage limited to these islands, or do you take yourself off to sunnier climes from time to time?

O'Hallaran stares at me as he chews. Unlike many of his vagrant brethren he has a full set of teeth. He pauses before answering, as if evaluating the measure of my insincerity. I have travelled a fair bit across the continent, he says. And beyond.

Ah, I repeat: *the continent*. And how, if I may ask, does one make ends meet, while engaged in a lifestyle such as yours?

I make ends meet, says O'Hallaran, slowly. I make things ...

Really? I interrupt him. You *make* things? Trinkets? Jewellery? You peddle artefacts for sale to unsuspecting tourists and their offspring at the seaside?

No, I was going to say: I make things grow. I work the fields. I am an itinerant agricultural labourer.

No thieving or beggary then?

Now, to be fair, I am quite surprised at myself over the

68

attitude I have struck towards O'Hallaran. For all I know he is harmless, and has wandered into Morgan's field quite by chance, without any dishonest intentions, but the truth is I have not yet overcome my utter confusion over the tent. To my mind, the tent either belongs to Alice, or it belongs to O'Hallaran; and as far as I am concerned it belongs to Alice, and O'Hallaran is an interloper. But Alice, for reasons I am not yet able to fathom, seems to find it feasible, even quite reasonable, that the tent belongs as much to O'Hallaran as it does to her. Therefore I must be missing something. I can see no harm in pursuing the topic further.

Look, O'Hallaran, I say. I realise we haven't made a very good start. But, you see, I'm a bit confused about your tent. A bit *muddled up*, shall we say. You said it was a gift from someone who passed away. Might I ask who that person was?

O'Hallaran stops chewing. Why, of course, he says. It was a gift from the lady who used to live in this house. Miss Megan. And now, if you'll forgive me, I need to get my head down. It has been a long and tiring day. Thank you for the supper. It was most kind of you to invite me into your kitchen.

He stands, returns his chair to its place at the table, strides to the door, and steps out into the night.

16

Once again, I contrive to sleep in the green armchair. I want to feel swathed in Megan's protective aura. I try to make sense of all that has happened today but instead plunge into further confusion. From the moment of my return to Llys Rhosyn, to find Alice standing like a ghost in the drive, everything has the taste and semblance of a dream. (I say this to myself, that my current life feels like a dream, but this doesn't help, since my insomnia casts almost everything into doubt anyhow – waking life *is* like a dream.) I wonder again whether I should pay another visit to Dr Homfray. He was very kind when I first went six months ago. As I have said, he prescribed sleeping pills, along with some others for what he termed my 'anxiety disorder'. I took them but they didn't work. He prescribed another kind of drug, a stronger sort, and so on. Nothing worked, and I still have boxes of them left. I tried exercise, herbal remedies, deep breathing, meditation, masturbation, relaxing CDs. (A complete misnomer; there is nothing remotely relaxing about these recordings of waves breaking gently on the shore, birdsong, the music of the spheres. I might as well have listened to the sound of farm animals greeting the day, or horses breaking wind.) Where my insomnia was concerned, nothing worked. Nothing *works*.

I read recently of a man, a celebrated insomniac, who claimed that long periods without sleep amount to a tyranny of consciousness; that normal people, who sleep the prescribed number of hours, awake each day as though starting out on a new life, but that for the insomniac no such renewal can occur. Instead, the sleepless live in a continuum of consciousness, and while everyone else rushes toward the future, we insomniacs remain outside. We don't have a future to look forward to, because there is none, only the persistence of an intolerable present. The unconscious replenishes: it is, as an American novelist once remarked, 'a machine for operating an animal'.

Once the machine is broken, what becomes of the animal?

I stand up, walk over to a bookshelf and pick, almost (but not quite) at random, the *Pretiosa Margarita Novella* or 'The New Pearl of Great Price' by Petrus Bonus, a fourteenth-century treatise that complains about the elusiveness and impenetrability of alchemical jargon. By choosing such a book in this exhausted state, I convince myself I am opening up to the forces of entropy, allowing a place for the random to settle and nurture seedlings. However, my secret purpose is more effective, and whatever the pearls contained in Petrus' work, within minutes I am asleep, head slumped forward, reading glasses fallen from my nose onto the pages of the open book.

On waking, as so often occurs, I feel immediately refreshed and alert. For the first few seconds only, to be accurate, but for those few seconds I am irredeemably awake, super-conscious and endowed with fabulous sensory powers: I can hear the spider on the wall behind my desk weaving its silken thread; can hear, through the half-open window, the dew forming on the lawn outside; I can even hear the calibre of my own thought.

I also hear footsteps on the stairs ...

The door opens and Alice steps into the library. I glance at my watch: it is a quarter to four in the morning, again. A coincidence? An intentional manoeuvre on Alice's part? I experience a powerful sense that this moment has occurred, not once, but countless times before, and will continue to

71

repeat itself infinitely, the door opening with a gentle creak, Alice stepping cautiously across the portal, the striped pyjamas lending a play of innocence to the scene, but also – a most unwelcome association – somewhat reminiscent of those monochrome clips from one of the darkest times in human history ... how have I conjured that image?

I greet her with a nod.

Couldn't sleep? I ask, putting aside my book, as though clearing a space for her.

She shakes her head and, folding her arms, walks toward the fire, which has burned quite low. May I? she gestures at the smoking hearth. First she stabs at the fire's entrails with the poker, then lays a few pieces of kindling across the glowing embers and waits for them to take light before carefully laying down two fresh logs. She replaces the poker and settles in her customary position on the sheepskin rug. And although Alice has given no indication that the subject has been playing on her mind also, I return at once to the theme that is obsessing me.

If Megan gave you the tent, she can't also have given it to O'Hallaran. And if she gave away two tents of exactly the same kind, then what has happened to yours?

She didn't make two tents, says Alice. There is only one tent.

There is only one tent, I repeat, pedantically. I have been trying to get my head around this notion all night, without a great deal of success.

Yes, she says. One tent.

But presumably, I persist, O'Hallaran, wherever he was yesterday morning, packed up his tent, put it in his rucksack, and arrived here in the afternoon. Then he put up his tent in exactly the same place that you had left your tent. The same tent, if you are to be believed. And nothing about the *logistics* of the thing – the pitching of a tent where a tent already exists – quite apart from the simple *logic* of it, strikes you as weird?

Oh, it's weird all right, says Alice, reaching down to fondle the ears of her canine chum, who has followed her into the library and settled at her side. I sit back in the armchair by the carved fireplace, sling my legs over the armrest. The fresh logs have now caught and are blazing in the grate. Shadows flicker across Alice's face, the reflected flames deepening the red in her hair.

I never said it wasn't weird, she repeats.

But its weirdness is not sufficient to make you question the whole sequence of events? How, for instance, Megan managed to give, as a gift, the same tent to two separate people?

Hmm, she says. Alice is smiling, while attempting to look thoughtful. This conflict of expression aptly encapsulates the ambivalence I myself am feeling. I am not sure whether she is messing with me, or flirting with me. Mixed messages, I am coming to realise, are part of the fun of hanging out with Alice.

She leans an elbow on my knee, and looks up at me, face resting on her forearm. She explains that the previous evening she had observed, from her bedroom window, the little scenario beside the tent, realised that something was amiss, and had gone out to the garden in receptive mood, determined not to act surprised as – she says – 'it can be dangerous to meddle with the tent's output'. *Output*, she says. She is aware, she tells me, that the tent can unleash 'mysterious things' and she didn't want to leap to conclusions about O'Hallaran. But what she doesn't tell me is how, after leaving me on the stairway, and taking a bath, she managed to transmute from a sickly, feverish girl into the healthy, composed woman who walked in on my argument with O'Hallaran.

Listen, says Alice, folding her arms now on top of my knee, and resting her chin on her wrist: why don't you have a proper chat with him, with O'Hallaran? See whether he's prepared to give you his story. You weren't particularly nice to him earlier. In fact, you were horrid. Perhaps you should give him the opportunity to explain himself. And maybe he knows something about the tent that we don't.

By 'we', she presumably means herself, as I know less than nothing about the damn thing.

The necklace with the scarab pendant swings at her throat as she looks up at me, awaiting my response. I am appalled at the magnitude of my feelings for Alice, and yet, when everyday reality is so cast in doubt, how can I trust the veracity of my own emotions? How can I be certain that she is even there, in flesh and blood, and she will not disappear, like a wraith, if I lean forward to kiss her?

17

The next morning, I determine to resolve matters with O'Hallaran. I will try to draw from him his story, and evaluate whether or not he is a trickster and a fraud, as I suspect, or whether – as Alice seems inclined to think – he should be given the benefit of the doubt. And if Alice is right, if it is the tent and not O'Hallaran that should be the focus of my concerns, what then?

I will have to deal with that matter as and when it arises.

At nine o'clock I venture over to O'Hallaran's camp and ask him to join me for breakfast, an invitation he accepts with alacrity, and without giving the least impression of having taken offence at my behaviour the previous evening.

Tell me, O'Hallaran, I say, once we are settled in the kitchen, over cups of coffee, I wish to be frank with you. Would you tell me a little of yourself? Answer me something that has been perplexing me all night?

I never, says he, could have any objection to providing an honest answer to an honest question. It is the other stuff that galls me, the assumptions and prejudices that attach to me, as it does to all homeless wanderers, or gentlemen of the road, a term you employed in reference to myself – not without irony, I recall – last evening.

Well, I say, you will perhaps forgive me a degree of circumspection, when within the space of a couple of days I receive into my house two strangers, each of them claiming ownership of the same item: a particularly unusual item, I might add, and one which both of these individuals claim was a gift from the same person, my late lamented Aunt

Megan. So my question is: how, precisely, did you acquire your blue tent from my aunt?

Very well, he says. And there is a long pause, as he rolls a cigarette, clearly much occupied by his thoughts. I give him all the time he needs, and I prepare another pot of coffee. It seems as though we are in it for the long haul.

– Many years ago, as I've told you, I worked as an agricultural labourer across southern Europe, travelling from place to place, picking up work on the cherries and peaches in the summer, on the grapes in autumn, the olive harvest and the oranges in winter. I usually worked in France in the summer and in Spain or Greece in the winter. And on the occasion I want to tell you about, I was working on the maize castration in the Gers, in south-west France. It was the month of August.

Perhaps I should explain something about working on the maize, on the *castrage*. If you imagine a maize or corn plant, around two and a half metres tall, the part you have to extract is like a bud in the fork of the plant, around shoulder height. You have to take it out to stop the next generation of maize from breeding an inferior crop; what the farmers call *bâtardes*, a term hardly requiring translation. Something to do with keeping intact a better strain of maize. Whatever. We were put into teams, *équipes,* as the froggies called them, like a football team. You'd work the rows together, don't lag behind, want to be on the best team, all that competitive bollocks. Well, me and my team, which included my mates Igbar Zoff and Rhys Lucas – degenerates the pair of them, but honest souls – we didn't give a shite about all that, we just wandered down the rows at our own pace, plucking the male genitals from the plants and tossing them away. And there was always some blasted team leader, *le chef d'équipe*, chasing after us, egging us on, getting us to hurry up … Tedious, like most manual jobs, I guess, though at least you're working outside and the weather's nice, if a little too warm at times... Anyway, I came upon the blue tent because I had something that the tent's owner wanted in exchange. An object that I had in my possession ...

An object? I interrupt.

A thing without a name, he adds, unhelpfully. A unique artefact. But in order to tell you how that happened, I need to give you some background, do you see? So, the day I found this object, I was working in the maize field, going up and down the rows, carelessly ripping the buds from the plants, when suddenly I felt my toes come into contact with something hard. I stooped to pick it up, a steel or silver cylinder – I never ascertained what metal it was made of – like a short length of piping, a tad smaller than a modern mobile phone, which I guess it resembled, *conceptually* – and he pauses for effect, as though pleased with the analogy – although a million times more powerful, more *informative*. And of course back in the eighties there were no such things as mobile phones, as we know them now. Anyways, it was about the size of my thumb (here he holds up his own stubby, gnawed, appendage) and even though I had no idea what the thing was, it immediately cast a kind of spell over me, as though it were, well ... *animate*. I held it in my hand, turning it over, and then I saw *inside it*. What I saw defied all rational explanation. At first I thought it was a trick of the light, but the closer I scrutinised the thing, the more I could see. It contained images, at first indistinct, then becoming clearer, of human faces, of streets, of entire cities, and of landscapes, grand and terrifying, of oceans and deserts and jungles and wild marshes, of animals and people of every kind. Everything was contained within its small screen. The whole universe, from every angle simultaneously, without distortion,

77

overlapping or confusion. The whole of history was in it, viewed from all perspectives. It was – he added – as you might imagine, incredibly heavy to hold in my hand.

I realised I was in possession of a rare, unique thing. A thing unheard of. Finding one in a maize field in the south-west of France, on an otherwise unremarkable August afternoon, provided a significant fillip to my day's labour.

A fillip indeed, I agree – although by agreeing with him, I know, I am only encouraging him in his folly.

It was like looking into – O'Hallaran pauses, as if choosing his words carefully – *the standing still of recorded time*.

I am impressed by his audacity.

No mean achievement then, you finding one like that in a field, I tell him. I think we have established that.

I didn't mean to brag. I only wished to convey the quality, or measure, of my amazement.

You have, I assure him.

So, he continues, after my initial reaction of bewilderment, to be sure – and what with the leader of our *équipe*, a fuckwit of the first order named Alphonse hurrying us up about our tasks, telling us to get on with the next row – I slipped the cylinder, heavy as it was, inside my trouser pocket. I won't say I forgot about it – how could I? – but, you know, out of sight out of mind, so I kept it hidden away and got on with the job.

That day, as it happens, was my birthday, the fifth of August. I decided the silver cylinder was some kind of a gift from Providence, that I had been blessed by the gods. There was no other way to get my head around it.

I had arranged with some friends, Lucas and Zoff and one or two others, Anto Walker from County Wicklow and Hubert Tsarko from Liverpool, all of them, like me, itinerant labourers, to go out to a certain bistro in Saint Mont, a restaurant not of the highest cast – that would have been way beyond our means – but a decent enough little eatery, where they serve duck in all its many guises, almost to the point of the ridiculous – hoisted by their own canard, you might think, if you will permit me the joke – (O'Hallaran seems to be enjoying himself far too much). They offer, he says, on the regular menu, duck with French fried potatoes, duck with chestnuts, duck with orange, duck in an Armagnac marinade …

Go on, I say – I get it. They served a lot of duck.

Quite so. In short, we had a good dinner. We all ate plenty of duck and drank sufficient of the wine, if not to excess. As we left the restaurant, whose name escapes me, a great fatigue entered my bones. The long hours in the fields under the blazing sun, followed by beers, then several *ricards*, all that heavy food, a surfeit of duck, an abundance I am sure, of bad jokes with old drinking buddies, and the good Madiran wine, a couple of Armagnacs to finish off, no wonder I was tired. The others, Lucas, Zoff, Tsarko and Walker – they sound like a firm of accountants, do they not? – were all in favour of setting off back to the town of Riscle, where we were based, and the Café du Soleil, our regular retreat, for a nightcap, but I said to them to go on ahead without me. You see, there was a lane leading up a small incline to the right of the restaurant, and twenty metres up the hill was a patch of green, and an eminently serviceable bench, which I thought I might utilise for a little nap before following my friends back to the café in Riscle, which was at a distance of five kilometres from Saint Mont. So I lay down to have a kip, and when I woke up, fully refreshed, I idled back down the road. It was a glorious summer's night, so I decided to walk, even turning down a lift from a car driven by some local farm workers, and eventually arrived in Riscle. And this is where things start to get uncanny.

79

When I got to the Café du Soleil, there was no sign of Zoff, Lucas and company, which was a little strange, but I ordered myself a beer anyway, and sat at a table outside on the pavement. The café was busy, as it always was during the *castrage*, especially during the evening. I had been there for five or ten minutes when a white BMW pulled up outside the church across the street and my friends piled out, expressing considerable surprise at seeing me there, sitting outside the café. Why, they said, you just set off up the hill for a late siesta, what are you doing here? According to their story, no sooner had they left me outside the Saint Mont bistro than a car stopped for them, driven by one of the more affluent *producteurs*, whizzed down the lane to Riscle at a cracking pace, and deposited them outside, as I had just witnessed. It would have been a *physical impossibility*, according to my friends, *for me to have arrived at the café before them.* Yet here I was, having had a short rest, walked five kilometres, and then waited at the café long enough to smoke a cigarette and drink a beer.

Well, of course, I had no explanation for my miraculous appearance, but then I hadn't told them about my find: I knew straightaway that the magic cylinder had a role in this mind-bending act of transportation. I can't tell you how I knew, I just did. And by my friends' startled declarations, I knew that their account was true, at least according to the regular laws of physics, and that I, despite leaving St Mont at a time significantly *after* them, had somehow contrived to arrive here in Riscle *before* them, as if the time I had spent sleeping on the bench at Saint Mont and walking between the two villages had simply been wiped out, gone, or else had taken place in another, parallel or alternative existence. I decided, foolishly, I now realise – and in spite of an inclination to conceal – to let my friends in on the secret, which I had until then, and throughout the course of dinner, kept from them. Fishing in my trouser pocket, I pulled out the cylinder and displayed it, my hand extended. The thing shone bright under the street lighting. Rhys Lucas stared intently at the cylinder, and Igbar Zoff, on tiptoe (he was a small man), gazed over Lucas' shoulder, sceptical at first, but nonetheless I could soon tell that the object had cast him under its spell also. Looking into it, they each individually – as they later told me – saw their own lives flash by, and the lives of all that had come before them and will come after them. My friends' faces were absorbed, their eyes enraptured by the marvellous things they could see in the silver cylinder, those fleeting, crowded images of all history, in all places.

For the first few days I was over the moon, I was Master of the Universe, and I shared my find with my friends, allowing them to glimpse its wonders, but then gradually, over the following two weeks, I became defensive about the thing, and guarded it jealously. I descended into a terrible depression. I stopped speaking, at least I stopped speaking to anyone or anything other than the silver cylinder, to which I murmured softly, as to a lover. My friends could no longer tolerate me and they left. Zoff and Lucas tried to talk me into coming with them – they were off to Spain with their earnings, for a beach holiday – but I knew that they were all consumed with envy, and just pretending to be nice, and that, really, all four of them were sick to death of me. I knew that for sure. I spent all my time consulting my cylindrical treasure, watching the events of history unfold within its small yet infinite space, marvelling at the revelation of things to come, and of things that might have been – for it soon became apparent that the wonderful object contained all possible stories, and not only those that took place, as it were, in actual fact. However, what the magical object could *not* do, which differentiated it from some kind of genie or oracle, was inform me about my present circumstances, or enable me to act on the information it provided. It could show me outcomes, but I had nothing to trace them back to, if you see what I mean, no way of telling whether its projections of the future were any more reliable than its representations of the past. It mixed facts with fiction. It showered me with images of every kind. Thus I could see the world, for instance, from the point of view of Roger the gimp, who spent each morning sipping his Armagnac while gazing at Mimi's cleavage; could witness the infidelities of the town rugby team's coach, Jean-Pierre; participate in the bizarre existential enquiries of the postwoman, Aurélie; share in the dreadful fear of death that tormented the school caretaker, Fréderic; recoil at the paedophilic fancies of old Pane, the *patissier*. But were these things real, or merely reflections cast up by the imaginings of these protagonists? I must confess, the magical screen often seemed to home in on truly vile and ugly things. Unless that's what it found most salient about human beings. Or unless it adjusted its revelations to suit the mind of the voyeur – a possibility that would not reflect well on me, I'm afraid. And though I could see all these things, and more, I was impotent to change any of it. It permitted only a detached observer. At the slightest inclination of the observer to take action, the screen, as it were, went blank. It knew, you see: it could read my mind.

So, I stayed in Riscle long after the *castrage* had finished, spending my earnings on drink, and passing long hours staring at my small treasure, lost in a terrible melancholy at all these grand and lowly – at times very lowly – worlds, which I could see, but never know.

One late September morning I was sat at my usual table in the Café du Soleil, sipping my third *pastis*, and beginning to enter that zone of unremitting self-pity familiar to all drinkers

82

of *pastis*, when an elegant and rather striking woman – a woman in her prime, let's say – entered the premises, ordered a large *café crème*, and deposited herself at the table next to mine. Being of a sociable and friendly disposition, in spite of my depressed state, I returned the French greeting, delivered, on her part, fluently, though in an unmistakably British accent, and I asked her, in English, whether she was on holiday. She replied that she had been staying with an old friend and colleague way to the east of Riscle, towards Toulouse, and that she was motoring (yes, she used the verb 'to motor') back to Britain, to Wales, though heading first for Paris, where she would be spending a week with other friends. It began as one of those casual conversations that take place between travellers, the lady polite and forthcoming, myself (regrettably) veering towards the sentimental, if not actively lachrymose. You see, the object had rendered in me an acutely distressed emotional state. I had begun to think ever more keenly of it as an animate presence. I doubt whether I would otherwise have responded quite so thoroughly to the lady's questioning, had not my secret treasure reduced me to this pathetic pass. But when she asked me what was causing me such distress I told her everything; I blurted out that I had found something of inestimable value, something so precious that I barely had time to register my immense good fortune, and yet now it had turned on me, and although I valued it as much as ever, I feared for my sanity.

The lady asked what manner of object I was referring to.

I struggled for a moment. Should I confess to this stranger that I was in possession of what was, in all probability, a fictional, even a *literary* object? What on earth would it mean to her, or to *most people*, to be told that I owned an object capable of displaying the entire contents of the universe? But I sensed – and was, it transpired, correct in this assumption –

that this lady was not to be confused with *most people*. She had about her a quickness, softened around the eyes by a kindness and gently subversive humour and was transparently sympathetic to people such as myself; the drifters and the shiftless, the uncommitted, those of us who are led – for good or for bad – by our imaginations, and who resort to reality only when all else fails.

So yes, I confessed to this person, who was of course your Aunt Megan, that I was, albeit by accident – if the concept of accident has any meaning in such a context – in possession of a magic cylinder that contained worlds within it. Her expression changed from one of civil concern for a suffering fellow-creature to one of absolute and undivided attention. Whether as a psychiatrist fascinated by marginal and occult phenomena (as I later discovered she was) or out of simple curiosity, she appeared profoundly impressed by my account of the object for which I had no name, and of the way it had taken over my life, even to the extent of ruining long-standing friendships with my travelling companions.

Megan then suggested that we order lunch. She was hungry, and would be happy to cover for me also. I think, perhaps, she was concerned that, after my fifth *pastis*, I was going to become hopelessly maudlin and unintelligible; in any case I had not eaten properly for days and I needed some solid fuel inside me, or *soakage*, as we say in County Cork.

Of course, Megan had the restraint not to ask to see it immediately, but during the meat course (duck, needless to say) I reached into my pocket and showed her the silver cylinder. Just as my erstwhile companions had been, she was transfixed. She gazed intently into its depths for a good long while, and although in no hurry to give it back, she didn't linger either. Her eyes were alight when she returned it to me, and she appeared to have come to some kind of a decision.

Toward the end of our meal, over coffee, Megan said she would like to suggest an exchange; a gift of something, if not of equal value – for who can value the inestimable? – then at least of considerable interest, and less damaging to a person of my evident sensitivity.

Obviously, I could not help interjecting here, with a sour chuckle.

O'Hallaran ignored my sarcasm, and continued.

She had, in her car, she said, something which also possessed rare and remarkable attributes. Would I be willing to consider accepting from her, in exchange for the burdensome silver cylinder, a tent that she had sewn with her own hands: would I have any use for it?

What, I ventured to ask, was the value of this tent? I mean, other than providing shelter and a degree of simulated domesticity for its owner? I had possessed tents in the past, but was not a great fan. I suffered from a kind of claustrophobia within the tight confines of a tent. I would prefer, I said, to sleep out under the canopy of stars, if you'll forgive the grandiosity of the expression.

The value of the blue tent is only discernible to its occupant, Megan told me. I cannot advise you in what ways, specifically, it will be of benefit to you. It may cause you to doubt various certainties you have held close all your life, but my guess is that you and the tent will get along famously and, considering the suffering that your mysterious find appears to be causing you, it would be more than a fair swap.

Looking back on it now, it was rather like being offered – by a benevolent dealer, if there ever were such a thing – a wonderful new drug, one which, like the silver cylinder itself, harboured untold mysteries and the promise of ecstatic revelations. In other words, she presented me with the ultimate sales pitch of all the illusory highs bought by countless poor sods of every generation that ever walked the earth.

Did I detect an edge of bitterness to O'Hallaran's voice?

I was beginning to reconsider him, and if not exactly warming to him, at least regarded him with rather less hostility than before. Not on account of his ludicrous tale, but because of his vulnerability in the telling of it. All of which might have been a part of the blarney, of course – but I was, at the very least, willing to give him a chance.

So, I say to him, what happened next?

Well, she paid for the meal, and then took me out to her car. A grand old Mercedes convertible, not the Estate, which I see you have inherited. Better suited to the sun-kissed roads of the south, wouldn't you agree? She opened the boot and pulled out the tent in its beautiful bright embroidered bag. I am not a sentimental man, you understand. I have an emotional streak, particularly when I have taken drink, but I immediately recognised the tent as a thing of beauty. I told Megan that I wanted to pitch it right away, and asked if she would be willing to help me. She replied, rather mysteriously, I thought, that the tent needed to become accustomed to its new owner, and that while she would be happy to do as I asked, she thought it better if I set things up myself, so that the tent 'shed her traces', and 'absorb the personality' of its new owner. And then, she suggested, without a hint of embarrassment, that it might 'help things along' if we slept in it together for a night or two – and she was using the term 'slept' in its colloquial as well as its literal sense: the tent needed to loosen its adherence to Megan's preoccupations and moods, since, she explained, this was a very personal kind of tent, and treated everyone who entered it in a very different manner. The whole point of the tent, she explained to me, its *raison d'être*, was that it would, eventually, find its own destiny; it was not bound to a single individual forever, but would, in the meantime, help shape the destiny of whoever owned it – meaning, for now, I guessed, myself.

And time has proved her right. It is now over thirty years since I acquired the blue tent from Megan. I have travelled everywhere with it. I might even say the tent has taken me along with it, wherever *it* has travelled. Mine has been a curious existence. I heard of Megan's death only two weeks ago, but I hastened here, to pay my respects in whatever way I might. It seems that doing so has proved rather more complicated than I envisaged. The tent, I may as well confess to you, has been playing up for a while now. The nearer we got to its place of origin the more disorienting became its whims and its curious little deceits. I thought I had better pitch camp here and find out what was going on.

And now, I say, do you know what is going on?

That, says O'Hallaran, is difficult to answer. Although, I appreciate, that is what you are most concerned to know. I understand your distrust of me, and I also understand from what you said last night that your friend Alice was also in possession of a tent, a very similar, if not identical tent. But as for finding out why the tent behaves in the way it does, what the tent *thinks* even – though clearly I do not mean this in any literal way – that is quite beyond my understanding. It is a measure of the tent's independence that it sometimes takes decisions that seem entirely perverse. Having been introduced to the tent by its creator in the manner that I did, I have come to accept its ways, but that is not to say I have not encountered the occasional setback. A couple of times the tent has taken offence at the particular spot I have chosen to pitch camp, and has moved – either with me in it or not – to a distance of many miles. You can perhaps imagine my vexation on waking within sight of the walls of Sarajevo, beside the humble Miljacka, having camped down, the night before, on the banks of the mighty Danube. But worse still was the time the tent simply took off without me. I spent three months tracking it down, pitched on a remote peninsular by the Black Sea. It was not a pleasant experience retrieving it.

I can imagine, I say, although really I cannot.

I'm content, for now, to indulge O'Hallaran. But the idea of a tent taking off of its own volition seems utterly insane to me, like a story from *The Thousand and One Nights*.

18

Over the next few days, O'Hallaran immersed himself in the daily activities, such as they were, at Llys Rhosyn, pottering around and making himself useful. In other words, he settled in, without actually moving in. He helped out enthusiastically with Alice's gardening projects. The two of them busied away in the greenhouse, planting seeds and cultivating tomatoes, while O'Hallaran, ruddy son of the soil, dug up the adjoining vegetable garden with a plan to planting rows of potatoes. You invite an Irish tramp to pitch his tent in your garden and sooner or later you'll all be on a diet of salted spuds, he joked, oblivious to the fact that I had not in fact invited him to do anything of the kind. From where I worked in the library, attempting to decipher my aunt's arcane texts, I would frequently hear peals of laughter emanating from the greenhouse. I assumed the two of them were sampling Megan's crop of wacky baccy. I could picture them lighting up and puffing away in there, oblivious to any worries. What a felicitous turn for O'Hallaran, I thought, to wind up at a remote country estate with a lovely young woman and a limitless supply of ganja. But in this respect, I probably did the fellow an injustice. True, I endured the occasional stirrings of jealousy as I imagined them cavorting among the tomato plants, but I did not seriously consider O'Hallaran a threat in this respect, and I intuited that any expression of possessiveness towards Alice on my part would meet with her disapproval. Indeed, I resigned myself to O'Hallaran, as one might to the weather, or a cough.

I had changed. I was curious, and realised I had even been rather bored by my solitary existence. I was willing to tolerate

O'Hallaran. I wanted, I think, to see what was going to happen next. Because, almost in spite of myself, I had become convinced of the intrinsic mystery of the tent, I was at least willing to be taken in by its mythology. As long as the blue tent was pitched there, almost anything might occur. So I watched and waited.

I continued not to sleep. I continued failing to acquire the minimum requirement for sleep in adult humans. I continued to experience the passage of night and day as a cranky experiment in staying awake. I had no idea of, had forgotten the simple beauty of, a refreshing night's slumber. I was confined to the downstairs, apart from trips to the bathroom and occasional sallies to my bedroom for a change of clothes. I had long since given up even attempting to sleep in the room in which I had first installed myself, the poignantly misnamed 'master' bedroom. It remained silent and empty, my clothes carefully folded away in the wardrobe, a pair of slippers dutifully placed at the edge of the bedside table, the bed linen undisturbed.

There was something else, which I found hard to articulate, but all the more distressing for that reason. At first I thought I was being neurotic, but it was almost as if I were becoming the outsider at Llys Rhosyn. After all, the other two had a common bond as guardians of the blue tent, whereas I had no such credentials. If for them the blue tent had served as a home, for me it had merely been a portal for their respective appearances. As my insomnia persisted, blighting my capacity for rational thought, I was not sure who was a part of whose story; who, as it were, had slipped into the folds of whose fiction. And at the centre of all this confusion lay the blue tent. As I had learned when waking inside it last time, before O'Hallaran's emergence, there was a sinister side to the tent, and it made me afraid. My curiosity about the tent became tinged with paranoia.

Within a week of his arrival, to my consternation, O'Hallaran had befriended not only Alice, but our neighbourhood fox, that curious little scavenger, the one whose passage across the lawn and down the drive I had happily been observing throughout the spring.

In the evenings, we took to sitting out by the big French windows leading from the library, with an aperitif: wine or cider for Alice and O'Hallaran, water or fruit squash for myself – I told them I had an allergy to alcohol, which was true, after a fashion. With the coming of summer, Alice informed me, taking an aperitif *al fresco* was a civilised thing to do. It was while we were sitting on the patio that O'Hallaran had taken to calling out to the fox as it passed by on its evening sortie, picking its way down from the woods, pausing at the edge of the lawn where the trees began, lifting a forepaw or cocking its head to one side, checking out the territory.

Foxy, he would call, in his benign drawl (the choice of sobriquet was typically inane) and the fox would stop in its tracks, sniff the air, and – to my astonishment, the first time it happened – wander over to where we were sitting in the hope of being thrown some titbit or other; an olive, a piece of salami, a few potato crisps. O'Hallaran would continue to speak to the fox, coaxing and uttering endearments, until it actually came up to us, placed its front paws on the table edge in the manner of a circus dog, and nudged the wooden bowl of crisps onto the floor with its snout, scattering the contents, which it then picked off, item by item.

I had, as I have mentioned, admired the fox from a distance, had envied him his regular patrols of the grounds, had even, I now realised, wished for his companionship, or some kind of kinship with him. He was, after all, my nearest neighbour. But I had lacked the practical sense or initiative to simply call him over and offer him some crisps.

And there were other ways in which O'Hallaran provoked my jealousy: not, I must emphasise, in any way that reflected badly on him – only on me. He had a way of getting things done simply and effectively, which I have never been capable of. His facility with manual work, the fact that he could *fix* things, the catch on the larder door, which had never closed properly – a perennial irritation which, however, I would never have thought of repairing, or been able to – and the discovery and use of a well, of whose existence I had been vaguely aware, but had never bothered to investigate or utilise. O'Hallaran had uncovered the well, and had set up a primitive pulley system whereby a bucket could be lowered and water brought up for use in the adjacent kitchen garden, thereby saving multiple trips to the kitchen or the acquisition of a garden hose. These small practical achievements were apparently a matter of instinct for O'Hallaran. What was worse, he set about them with a modesty and accomplishment that never drew attention to himself. He was, on the contrary, unobtrusively useful, something I have never been.

At Alice's request, and with my approval, O'Hallaran constructed a fenced area near the vegetable patch, which provided a kind of run for the dog whenever he became too excited, or demanding of attention. Fortunately, this was not often necessary, as under Alice's supervision the young sheepdog seemed to be happy and obedient, and she quickly had him housetrained. His limp had gone and his name shortened from Ketamine to Keto, which was only to be expected. But if we were eating outside, we would sometimes put him in the run. It was from this vantage point that he observed the first visit of the fox to the table; barking at first, but then merely curious, and eventually complacent, as though accepting Foxy as one of the furnishings in this benevolent new life away from Morgan's more Spartan regime.

The days became weeks, and the spring turned to summer, and almost without my noticing, I found myself living in a kind of chaste *ménage à trois* with my uninvited guests, the dog thrown in.

I continued to watch and wait.

19

There was a significant difference in the way I treated my two visitors. I had invited Alice to sleep in the house within twenty-four hours of making her acquaintance. O'Hallaran, on the other hand, never received such an offer. Nor, I think, would he have accepted.

Put simply, he seemed more suited to the outdoor life, and consequently I didn't question him continuing to live in the tent, rather than in the house. It made sense. He had lived in his tent for thirty years, by his own account. Alice, by contrast, only ever claimed to have slept in her tent occasionally, on trips abroad or excursions or holidays. The rest of the time, she told me, she stayed at her mother's place in Devon, or with a girlfriend in France, the daughter of Megan's best friend, Zoë, whom Alice had met through my aunt.

If O'Hallaran had moved in, it would have felt like a crowd to me, accustomed as I was to having the whole house to myself, but the subject never actually arose, since O'Hallaran seemed happy with his nomadic lifestyle, and after sharing an evening meal with us, which he would frequently prepare himself – he was a competent if unadventurous cook – he would take his leave and retire to the tent.

And I continued in my struggle with insomnia, in the armchair in my library, or else stretched out on the sofa in the living room, where I would watch the DVDs from Megan's collection – *Blithe Spirit*, *The Red Shoes*, *The Man from Morocco*. Sometimes Alice would join me, and we would snuggle up on the sofa together like brother and sister.

The fact that O'Hallaran was made to feel so welcome was

largely Alice's doing. As she had explained to me in the library, on the night of his arrival, she believed that O'Hallaran was bound to possess a better grasp of the tent's idiosyncrasies than she herself did. If this were so, I asked her, a week after his arrival, following a late night viewing of *The Life and Death of Colonel Blimp*, what had she learned?

She seems puzzled by the question. Not offended exactly, but veering that way, put out by the directness of my question. Why did I want to know? For the same reason, I say, as I had wanted to know when he first arrived, namely, that I could not get my head around the fact that both of them appeared to be in possession of the tent, which was indubitably the *same* tent, and yet neither of them considered it strange that the other person claimed to own the tent.

But I never claimed to *own* the tent, says Alice. I said it was a gift from Megan, and that I had travelled with it, and that I slept in it. But did I say I owned it? I don't think so.

You are being disingenuous, I say: you arrived at the house in possession of the tent, and O'Hallaran arrived in exactly the same way three days later. When we first met, you accused me, if I remember rightly, of coming into 'your home'.

That may be so, she says. I was the temporary resident. But my arrival here was distinct in every way from O'Hallaran's. His long term residency of the tent makes a crucial difference.

So what have you found out? I say, ignoring her evasions. After all, you spend enough time together in the greenhouse.

Alice looks at me in a dark way.

Listen, she says. You're making too much of this. You're acting as though there were some kind of conspiracy. There is no conspiracy. I don't understand how the tent works, and I don't really think that O'Hallaran does either, even after all these years. It's a mystery. But we ... you, are always wanting rational explanations for everything. Why don't we just go along with it instead? The tent brought you and me together, and now O'Hallaran has joined us. It's not likely to be a permanent arrangement, if that's what you're worried about. O'Hallaran will be moving on. It's what he does, it's in his blood. And I will too, I am sure.

Something shifts within me again. I cannot bring myself to look her in the eye. You don't have to, I say. Move on, I mean. You can stay if you want, for as long as you need.

20

We assemble on the patio the next evening. It has been wet and overcast for much of the day, but by six o'clock, when we convene for drinks, it is fine, the sky almost cloudless, the sun just beginning its descent beyond the hills to the west. There is a lot of avian activity above the woods, the crows cacophonous around the treetops. I wonder about the crows, the din they make, their horrible communal lifestyle. I turn away. Something about the crows sickens me.

O'Hallaran has made a ratatouille, which is simmering on the stove in the kitchen. It is now almost three weeks since his arrival. While I have, thus far, been easy-going as to the exact nature of O'Hallaran's visit, I am beginning to feel uncomfortable about the length of his stay. True, he has been no bother – indeed, as I have noted, he has been most helpful about the place – but his very presence has had the unfortunate effect of inhibiting my relationship with Alice, which, I feel, was developing quite sweetly before she fell ill; before, that is, the appearance or intrusion of O'Hallaran. Besides, for all I know – although he has outwardly been the picture of propriety in this respect – he may have similar ambitions for himself. And he would, if I have read his character correctly, be considerably more forthright in his approach than I seem capable of, in spite of the considerable age difference. (While I am a decade older than Alice, O'Hallaran is almost two decades older than me.) So, since I have no intention of broaching the subject by direct means, I do wonder whether they have met before.

I ask him, as this has not been clarified since our interview over breakfast on the first full day of his visit, whether or not he had any further dealings with Megan, since meeting her in the Café du Soleil in Riscle in, when was it, nineteen eighty something?

He takes a drink and smacks his lips in a vulgar fashion.

I'm afraid I did not, he says, much as I would have liked to. Other than during the first few days following our exchange of goods, as it were. And he winks, the scoundrel.

He takes a long slurp of his drink, a Château Margaux. Alice has uncovered several cases in the store-room off the kitchen. What on earth is she doing, making available an almost unlimited supply of top quality wines to an individual accustomed to, and quite happy with, plonk or rough cider? My mood is not the best. I fear the evening is not getting off to a good start.

But the two of you – I gesture at Alice – had not met in all those years?

No, says O'Hallaran, I never had that pleasure, until this occasion.

And you, I say to Alice, feeling like a police interrogator, Megan never spoke to you of a Mr O'Hallaran?

Oh no, she says. Nor did I have any notion of his existence. She takes a puff of her roll-up, and leaning her head back, exhales, seemingly bored by the drift of my questions.

I have a suspicion they are both lying.

Don't be like that, I say. I'm curious. After all, you are guests here, and turned up within a couple of days of each other. It's intriguing.

Quite so, she says, as all coincidences are. My dear, you seem so uptight. You are anguishing unnecessarily about the tent. Unlike Megan, who always took things as they came.

No, I say. That's where I think you're mistaken. Megan might have given the impression of taking things in her

98

stride, of being terribly laid back and so forth, but in fact I believe she planned everything out in great detail before deciding on anything of consequence.

Really? says Alice. What makes you think that?

Well, her library for one thing. I do not think her library is the creation of a person who left anything at all to chance.

Go on, she says.

Much of my aunt's library consists of works by ancient alchemists, some of them in English, many in Latin, along with countless commentaries by scholars written in English, French, German, Spanish. There is also a substantial section of works in Arabic. I wasn't even aware Megan knew Arabic. Did you know she could read Arabic? (Alice did not.) When I first arrived at Llys Rhosyn, there was a handwritten note on the desk, addressed to me, and left there by Megan. I quote from memory, having pondered its words a thousand times over the past year: *One book opens the other. Read many books and compare them throughout and then you get the meaning. By reading one book alone you cannot get it, you cannot otherwise decipher it.*

Well, she says, that's deep, but what does it mean, beyond the idea that everything is linked?

It reflects a way of thinking around things, I say. It sums up an attitude, a *modus operandi*. It says you cannot make any useful decisions or reach any valid conclusions until you have examined a problem from all quarters and come to an informed opinion. It also means, by extension, that you should not trust one person's judgement without putting it under scrutiny, and comparing it with the opinions of others: *compare them throughout and then you get the meaning*. It also, incidentally, convinced me that I needed to read every book in the library – in the languages I could read, at least – before deciding what I was going to do next. With my life, that is. So that is what I am doing. In fact, that is all I do. It is what I am engaged in doing. Reading every damn book in the library. Not just the alchemical *esoterica*, although there appears to be a surfeit of that. But the library is extraordinarily laid out: I seem to know, by a series of clues laid down by the book I am reading at any time, which volume I must read next.

Alice is silent for a moment. Maybe she is wondering how she fitted into Megan's larger scheme of things, whether my aunt had applied the same principle to the running of her life, her friendships – and her protégée – as she had to her library. It was impossible to tell, from studying Alice's face. She might equally have been puzzling over her tomatoes, and how to protect them from bugs without using nasty chemicals, or wondering whether Foxy would make an appearance at our table tonight. I have to admit that I was devoid of any certainty regarding what Alice thought. There was a shifty quality to her facial expressions, which had begun, I am certain, the night that O'Hallaran arrived. Or was this my invention; an expression of my insecurity, or paranoia? How could I possibly pretend that I had learned how to read Alice in the three days I had known her before the arrival of the wretched O'Hallaran?

My concentration was waning. I put it down to lack of sleep, of course; but then I put most of my intellectual failings down to lack of sleep. And lack of sleep can't be responsible for everything. And then, in my hazy, fuddled way, I have what seems like a revelation: that I have lived inside the library this past year just as O'Hallaran has lived inside his tent, and, just as the library was a text – a *series* of texts – so was the tent. The only difference, and it was no small matter, was in how to read them, the texts and the tent. At that moment I have another one (another apparent revelation) and ask O'Hallaran:

If you've had the tent for so many years, it must have suffered the occasional damage; wear and tear. Tents get torn. Have you needed to repair it, ever?

The tent is very strong, says O'Hallaran. But it came with a repair kit that Megan presented me with that first day in the Gers. Strips of strong blue treated fabric, neatly folded in a blue canvas bag. Just in case, she said. The repair kit itself was inserted into a zipped pocket on the outside of the blue bag. All of it, but all of it – tent, bag, pockets, as blue as a baboon's arse. The fact is I've never had to repair the tent. It has never been torn, even when it disappeared for a month. Immaculate it was, when I found it that time, on the shores of the Sea of Galilee. Why, says O'Hallaran, do you ask?

Well, I say – certain that in his previous account the tent had turned up near the Black Sea – I'm wondering whether the tent has consciousness. I'm wondering whether any damage to its surface structure causes malfunctioning of some kind. Or whether it has some self-repair mechanism, like a living organism.

Sheesh, says Alice. A living organism. A breathing Tardis. Brilliant!

I look at Alice closely. I cannot decide whether or not she is taking the piss. Now, why would she do that?

O'Hallaran chuckles. I like it, he says. I've actually wondered the same thing.

Lying bastard. He knows! At least, he's had thirty years to think about it without pretending to humour my wild guesses. And yet he continues to chortle away, maddeningly.

I acknowledge that my sentiments regarding O'Hallaran are by no means straightforward. Part of me wants to befriend him, to accept him willingly into the household, even, heaven forbid, in my brighter moments, under Alice's influence, I think of starting a small community: some would tend the land, planting vegetables and cultivating fruit trees (we have a small apple orchard, which Alice has tentatively suggested supplementing with cherry and plum); others, like myself, would study arcane texts and pursue a more intellectual, or spiritual agenda. In the evenings we would meet up on the patio and discuss the day's progress, or gather around the fire in winter. Like monks, or nuns. Or monks and nuns.

But who am I kidding? When have I ever wanted to live like that?

Am I being infected by some hideous hippy virus, some kind of delusion of a sharing, communal idealism? Is the appearance of O'Hallaran (and of Alice, let's be fair) just the beginning? Have I opened the gate to some kind of gathering of the happy clans to Llys Rhosyn? An influx of weirdos, who will talk to plants, use healing crystals, and believe a woodlouse may be someone's grandmother? Is this something that Megan actually planned, and set up in advance of her death, having befriended numerous waifs and strays in the course of her lifetime? And who knows: from O'Hallaran's account, she possibly had sex with other drifters like himself?

And what about the other, antisocial side of me, the personality I am struggling to hold in check? The side of me that wants to smash O'Hallaran's skull in with a shovel and ravish Alice among the tomato plants?

Which side am I most afraid of?

I have no idea what my face is doing, but Alice is peering at me strangely. She has rolled a cigarette and is proffering it in my direction. No, not a cigarette, a medium-sized joint. She pushes it towards me. Go on, she says, have a little smoke. It might help you relax. You look all tense.

God knows, you'd be tense, I think, if you had just glimpsed what was passing through my interior field of vision … but instead I accept the thing, mainly because she has caught me unawares and I have no ready reason to refuse. Besides, I don't want to look uncool, a lightweight, in front of O'Hallaran.

Although I suggested to Alice that I was no stranger to the weed, it was a lie. A good decade has passed since I last had a smoke, and even back then, in the loom of youth, I was never a connoisseur. I *am* a lightweight, which is why I don't drink, either. I get confused and disoriented far too easily on those rare occasions when I drink anything stronger than lemonade, and I come out in a rash, literally. And smoking, Christ, even smoking a cigarette sends my head all over the place. As for weed, I start thinking things that no sane person should be allowed to think, and saying things that no one should ever say, unless they want the world to lock them up and throw away the key.

I take a couple of quick puffs, to save face, and pass the damn thing on to O'Hallaran.

You know, he says, taking a slow drag, you could almost become self-sufficient here at Llys Rhosyn, if you put your mind to it. Everything you could ask for. Good soil, timber aplenty. You could convert to solar, for a start. Grow whatever you cared to. And if you wanted meat, these fields are thick with rabbits. Hopping about like there was no tomorrow.

I yawn, extensively. It irritates me that people like O'Hallaran always have to remind you of the potential for Edenic solutions, because they are never going to have responsibility for those decisions themselves, only give their ill-informed opinion, garnered from long years of living off others and doing sod all of any consequence. I heave a big sigh and nod my head. I realise I am going to have to say something boring in response, to keep the conversation going. It's what people do.

I'm sure, I say, that one might. One would need a certain amount of capital to get started though. *Blah blah.* Miraculously the joint has come back to me. I inhale more deeply, burning my tongue, and hand it back to Alice, which was apparently the wrong thing to do, as she passes it on to O'Hallaran without taking a puff. Have I offended the protocol of the shared spliff? This is why I hate these gatherings. How on earth did my alcohol-free cocktail hour turn into cannabis corner? Why do I let these things happen? Or, I think, with a shudder, maybe she hasn't taken a drag because she's afraid I have some vile contagious disease, and she doesn't want to take the risk. Maybe that is why she won't kiss me properly either. I have a patch of dry skin at the corner of my mouth, a slightly sore spot. She must think it is a Herpes, acquired through my having had carnal relations with some beast of the field, because I have so clearly not had sex with a woman for such a long time, it must be etched on my face, it must be tattooed across my forehead: *pussy-free zone.* Wait a minute. Did I *say* that last bit or think it? If I thought it then no one will have heard, will they? *Will* they? So, did I say it or think it? Saying things and thinking things are different. People cannot hear your thoughts. I'm sure I only thought it. In which case why is Alice looking at me in that way? Perhaps I did say it. Oh God.

O'Hallaran is suggesting we eat outside, since it is such a pleasant evening. I concur with a kind of grunting sound, such as a pig might make. No idea how that noise escaped my mouth. Consciousness has detached itself from my vocal chords, my trachea, my tongue, my lips. The latter feel as though they have been plastered onto my face by accident, by some slap-happy infant sculptor. The thought appeals to me and I suppress a violent desire to laugh out loud. I touch them, my lips. I put my hand to my mouth. I trace my finger along the upper lip and feel the soft down of my facial hair. I have not shaved for several days, but this is not a planned moustache, only self-neglect. I draw my middle finger slowly along the lower lip. It feels dry. I realise with horror that this rubbing of my lip, this gentle stroking back and forth, might look obscenely suggestive to any onlooker, unconscious though it is … But why am I doing this weird thing in front of Alice? What are my eyes doing, I wonder, as I unwittingly caress my lips? I pull my hand away and stand up too quickly, knocking over my drink of orange squash, and hurry into the kitchen, ostensibly to help O'Hallaran bring in some plates and cutlery, but really to get away from Alice before she sees through me completely, sees what a foul and lecherous creature I am. She calls after me that I have spilled my drink; yes, I call back, I'll fetch a cloth. In the kitchen I go over to the CD player and pretend to be choosing a disc. I find some jazz from Megan's collection, Bud Powell, and slip it on. O'Hallaran is collecting the saucepan with the ratatouille onto a tray along with dinner plates, a basket of bread, salt and pepper. I pick up a bottle of wine from the table, and fill an empty carafe with water from the tap. The water here is good. Soft water, from the hills. The room spins towards me, then recedes. I suffer an overwhelming desire to burst out laughing again, but manage to contain it. I pick up a corkscrew, a jar of mustard, the breadknife, and load them onto another tray. Must look useful in front of Brendan O'Hallaran. That's it. Brendan. That shall be his name henceforth, whether he likes it or not.

Outside, I unload my tray with a clatter. I whistle along to the music, abstractedly, but stop when I realise I am doing it. I know how irritating it can be when someone whistles or hums along to a song. I am not normally this self-conscious. Is this what marijuana does? Why on earth do people smoke the stuff, then? For pleasure? I can feel a certain physical glow, a suffusive warmth coursing through my bloodstream, but the feeling that I am being observed, that I am, in an uncomfortably real sense the object of the universe's scrutiny outweighs the sensation of wellbeing. My mouth is dry, and since I have spilled my orange squash and cannot be bothered returning to the kitchen and do not feel like drinking water, I pour a glass of wine. Yes, I decide that I fancy a glass, after all. Its sensual and musty flavours are a little overpowering at first, but once I have knocked back a glassful, I realise I rather like the taste. I top up my glass, offering a refill to Alice and O'Hallaran also. I smile at Alice, who smiles back.

What ho! I say, for absolutely no reason at all, other than to sound jolly. But of course, it doesn't sound jolly, it sounds quite retarded, as though I were some character from a Bertie Wooster story. I know, of course, that this is the effect I am making, but I am being *intentionally* anachronistic, so it doesn't count. I finally let out a cackle of violent, insane laughter, and spill ratatouille, which I have been ladling from the saucepan, onto my foot. Since I am wearing flip-flops, and the vegetable gloop is hot, it burns me. I hop up and down, waving the ladle, which splashes bits of tomato and onion and courgette over O'Hallaran's, I mean *Brendan's* head. He jerks back in his seat, affronted at first, then realises it is an accident and wipes himself with a serviette. All of this is over in a few seconds, but to me it feels as though I have been negotiating hostile terrain for an eternity, and am not sure I can sustain the tension. I collapse onto my seat, a nervous wreck. All this excitement has taken away my appetite. I pour another glass of wine instead, thinking it might help, and knock it back in one.

My, says Alice, you *are* thirsty. Something about her tone of voice reminds me of our first meeting, after I had sprinted down through the woods to follow her into the house, and she is back to being the sweet gypsy girl I first met, and less of the thoughtful sophisticate who appeared after her strange illness. I am overcome with longing and gaze at her like an imbecile. She passes me a dishcloth, probably to distract me, and so that I can wipe the spilled supper from my foot, but I can't be bothered. O'Hallaran is tucking into the food with his customary relish.

Sorry, I say to him, about the spillage.

Don't worry about it, he says, tearing bread from the loaf. He looks like a wild man, his hair a mess, his beard flecked with the stew, bits of which he has missed after my accident with the ladle. He doesn't care though. He certainly doesn't appear preoccupied by anyone else's opinion of him, or the way he looks. He is evidently more self-contained than I am, despite his poverty. He possesses Good Faith. I drink more wine, and dunk a slab of bread in my bowl, scooping up the juices. It is a delicious ratatouille. I say as much, complimenting the chef.

Easiest dish in the world, ratatouille, says O'Hallaran.

Heavens, we are getting along famously. What a merry gathering. I raise my glass to the other two, and suggest a toast. *To the Blue Tent*, I say, and all who travel in it. The Blue Tent, they both murmur, though not, I feel, with quite enough enthusiasm.

We clink glasses (but not I feel, with quite enough vigour).

Fuck it, what is the matter with these people? Where is their *jouissance*, their *joie de vivre*? Why don't they show a little more fervour?

My head is beginning to ache. Perhaps I have drunk the wine too quickly. I seem to be stuck in a tight repetitive circle, condemned to a pursuit of the same inane concepts, all of them made ridiculous by the language I choose to describe them, all of them concerning the blue tent. Maybe – by the law of opposites, as my addled brain informs me – speaking some more will help. Language, after all, is a form of action.

So I say: Damn it, O'Hallaran, I believe I am going to punch you on the nose.

I have always been horrified by the notion that intoxication, rather than unleashing random and irrelevant ravings, actually reveals the dark undercurrent of our true nature. But something is stirring in me, and rather than concealing or repressing my innermost desires – as I normally endeavour to do – what would happen if, as seems to be occurring at this very moment, I were to act on a fleeting impulse?

And yes, I do feel an intense desire to punch O'Hallaran on the nose. I start giggling idiotically at the thought of this, not so much the act of physical violence as the expression itself, the *words*, and the fact that I have uttered them. Even the fact that I have specified the exact portion of his physiognomy that I will be aiming for. O'Hallaran, meanwhile, is watching me curiously. He remains in a seated position, which tactically places him at a disadvantage, but he does not withdraw his gaze from me.

So, I say, how about it, you smooth-talking, red-nosed bastard? What do you say to a few rounds with a real champ? I begin sparring, shadow-boxing, making little spitting sounds with each imagined moment of contact. Phut phut, phut, I go, as I curl my left fist into jabbing hooks and pummel the air with straight rights, while dancing over the flagstones in deranged imitation of Mohammed Ali. I move in on O'Hallaran, punching and feinting around his head, phutting out my little exclamations as I make contact with each fantasy target.

Aw, come on now, says O'Hallaran. Sit down for a moment, won't ya. You're making me dizzy.

I am not certain of the precise sequence of events at this stage. All I remember is that the world sways around me, my head makes contact with something hard, and the sky collapses.

Time passes.

Zzzzzzzzzzzzzzzzzz.

Took a bit of a tumble there, you poor palooka.

I look up and the fox is standing at my feet, staring at me.

Did he speak? Did the fox address me, in a kind of mumbling badass Bronx accent, as though his mouth were full of gravel? Did Foxy call me a *palooka*?

I am caught between achieving full consciousness and digesting this unexpected development, when the fox starts licking my toes. Yes, Foxy really is there, gathering up the spillage from our dinner party, including lashings of ratatouille and a few loose strawberries, which lie abandoned about the ground. And then Alice is here too, leaning over me. O'Hallaran is clearing dishes from the table, whistling an old rebel song that goes: *Too ra lay, too ra loo, they're looking for monkeys up at the zoo, but if I had a face like you I'd join the British army*.

I move my legs and Foxy hops away, as if surprised that the object of his investigation is in fact animate. He stands at a distance and regards me warily before turning tail – a most felicitous expression in his case – and departs across the lawn.

I am glad the fox has gone. His continued presence, especially the possibility of his having spoken, was most vexing.

How are you now? says Alice. She is stroking my temples, massaging with gentle circular movements, perhaps believing that this will return some degree of life or intelligence to what remains of my mind. I have no idea whether it helps, but it certainly feels soothing. I think of asking her what happened, but I don't really care. I don't want to know.

I tell Alice I would like to move indoors. She asks whether I think I can walk. I say I can, but might need a little help. I am like a wounded hero. I lean on Alice, and together we wobble into the kitchen. Library, I command, and so we lurch through the hall and into the inner sanctum, while O'Hallaran, I am pleased to observe, busies himself with the washing-up. I plonk myself into the green armchair, and Alice pulls up a footstool, onto which, almost reluctantly, it seems to me, she lifts my feet. She throws a blanket around my shoulders, and leaves the room. Presently I hear her chatting to O'Hallaran in the kitchen. Within a few short minutes I have been transformed from blathering buffoon to needy invalid. Is this what I have brought upon myself? Am I turning into a victim of the tent's devices, as, quite possibly, Alice and O'Hallaran already are, in their different ways. I rest my head back on the cushion behind me.

Alice returns to the library, kneels down next to the fireplace and prepares a fire, twisting newspaper and arranging kindling. This feels right; a return to comforting ritual, one which is associated, for me, with that brief interlude of domestic serenity and newly forged friendship when Alice had just moved in. Nostalgia, I realise, for the very recent past. Nostalgia for something that has only just happened.

Later that night, after Alice has gone to bed and O'Hallaran has returned to his tent, I take a long bath, soaking in the big enamel tub with a warm flannel over my face. It is while I am lying there, absorbed in dark thoughts, that the obvious solution occurs to me. If O'Hallaran is causing me distress, if his appearance has coincided with an inexplicable shift in my own personality – and a corresponding detachment from me on the part of Alice – and if I don't have the resolve or the courage to ask him to leave immediately, I must resort to more roundabout means. I must get inside the tent. Firstly, because if I wish to find out more about O'Hallaran, I need to look through his personal effects, to see if there is anything that incriminates him in some way, that I can *use against him*. Secondly – and more importantly – since he appeared almost immediately after I had ventured into the blue tent for the second time, might it not transpire that (by the law of opposites, again) if I return inside the tent, O'Hallaran will disappear, or *be disappeared*?

The resolution fills me with hope, and with energy. I climb from the bathtub, wrap myself in a towel and wander back to the library, dripping bathwater over the parquet floor. It is three o'clock in the morning, but I am wide awake. I wander over to the tall bookshelves on the north wall and select, almost (but not entirely) at random, the *Aphorismi Urbigerani or Certain Rules, Clearly Demonstrating the Three Infallible Ways of Preparing the Grand Elixir of the Philosophers*.

21

The next morning O'Hallaran humiliates me further by not mentioning my behaviour of the day before. Somehow it would have been better if he had chided me good-naturedly for my feeble foray into the pugilistic arts, or teased me about my woeful lack of tolerance for minute quantities of cannabis and red wine, the effects of which, on a normal person, would have been negligible, and on a seasoned degenerate like O'Hallaran, would have been utterly inconsequential.

Instead he greets me cheerily from the kitchen door, and wonders if there is a cup of coffee to be had. If this represents a modest attempt not to be intrusive, then he fails, but I have no reason to refuse him hospitality, especially as I plan shortly to be rid of him.

Sorry about that caper last night, I say. The wine must have gone to my head, or something.

Oh, think nothing of it, says O'Hallaran. It was a blessing you knocked yourself out. Saved me from having to do it for you. *Ha ha ha*, he goes. And so he still finds it funny, the swine.

Over coffee O'Hallaran announces that he needs to go to the post office in town. I cunningly offer him the loan of the car, but he says he does not drive. My generosity does not extend to offering him a lift myself, for obvious reasons. Since Alice does not drive either (or does not volunteer to) he says he will walk. That is good, as it will take him at least four hours to walk to town and back. Even if he gets a lift from some passing motorist he will be away most of the morning.

With O'Hallaran safely off the premises, it's time for me to make my move. Outside, the weather is overcast and rain

112

threatens. Standing at the tent's entrance, on the edge of the field, I feel like an explorer at the point of entering remote and inhospitable territory, although I am more self-conscious and nervous than on either of the previous occasions. The first time – which Alice witnessed, unbeknownst to me – I was swept away, passing out in the swirling blue sea of the tent, and the second time I was simply exhausted, and had lain down to sleep. On this occasion, although I do not exactly have a plan, I have a pressing need to bring about a turnaround in my circumstances. Ideally this would be the removal of O'Hallaran from the vicinity of the house. If, as I have gathered, the tent can be amenable to the desires of its occupant, perhaps it will do as I wish. I know, from O'Hallaran's own account, that the tent has been 'playing up' of late, that it has been making difficulties for him. I flatter myself to think that perhaps, as the tent seems so very receptive to me, it is going through a change of allegiance. At the very least, it will come up with something; of that I am certain.

I open the front flap in authoritative manner, as though I mean business. As though I were unzipping my pants. It is important to let the tent know I am not to be trifled with. There is a black duffle bag lying alongside O'Hallaran's blanket. He has no sleeping bag, but this nice thick ethnic blanket, of Balkan or Slavic appearance, that I recognise from my previous visit. I rummage through the bag, and immediately find a yellowing photo of Megan as an attractive woman of middle age, in an ostensibly French village square (thereby coinciding with O'Hallaran's account of first meeting her back in the 1980s) and several photographs of persons unknown, and of O'Hallaran himself in a younger incarnation, with much longer hair, and a clutch of small notebooks, tied together with a plastic band, through which

113

I riffle. The handwriting is atrocious, and the notes are accompanied by a number of childish but entertaining drawings. If indeed the notebooks are his, he has an artistic side.

I replace the items in the duffle bag and attempt to focus my mind on making O'Hallaran go away. I visualise him alone, walking over an Arctic landscape. I imagine him picking his way across snow into the distance, becoming ever smaller, until his figure is a mere pinprick on the blurred horizon. I am then tempted to visualise a scenario in which a polar bear attacks and eats him, but retract the thought, suspecting that the tent may not take me seriously if my fantasies become too extreme. I lie back on the ethnic blanket and imagine diverse scenes in which the solitary figure of O'Hallaran vanishes into oblivion: I picture him disappearing, by turn, into the barren depths of a rocky desert, the yellow dunes of the Sahara, a bleak and cratered moonscape, and finally I have him alone in a small dinghy, way out at sea, the swell around him mounting, his tiny boat dwarfed by massive waves. This last visualisation has a strangely comforting effect and, rather than seeing the figure of O'Hallaran tossed on the crest of distant breakers, it is I myself who am in the boat, relaxed to the point of stupor, being carried to stupendous heights and dropped to abysmal depths at the mercy of the sea's heave and sway, while remaining entirely without fear. I feel once again the familiar inundation in deep blue, the folding in of sky and sea, my body utterly at the mercy of a great seething marine force, upon which I am carried, gently now, into the deepening folds of the indigo night …

It is Alice who wakes me. She has been looking for me all over, she says. When she could not find me in the library or anywhere else in the house, it occurred to her that I might be in the tent. I try to muster myself, but my body feels bruised and stiff. I crawl outside, and am relieved to find that it is only just past midday. O'Hallaran has not returned, Alice tells me, in answer to my question.

This piece of information does not console me, nor indeed do I register any emotion. I am indifferent to O'Hallaran, in a way that certainly was not the case before going inside the tent. Despite feeling physically knocked about (as though I really have been cast adrift in a storm-tossed dinghy), I know something is different, as though a mist has lifted. I am refreshed by my sleep, but also intellectually re-charged: detached and autonomous, much as I had been before O'Hallaran's appearance, but more so: I feel more assertive, more confident and, yes, more *manly*.

Why were you trying to find me? I ask, once I have zipped up the front flap.

Oh, she says ... I don't know. It just felt a bit strange with no one about. By the way, she says, what were you doing in the tent?

Sleeping, I say, evasively. One thing I have learned is that I invariably manage to fall asleep in the tent, so I went there for a kip.

Well, she says, I am pleased. I have a feeling you're going to need your strength, she adds, mysteriously, and she links her arm through mine as we walk back to the house.

22

In the kitchen we are sitting in silence, waiting for the coffee to brew, when there is a knock at the back door, and someone calls out Alice's name. Alice responds with a greeting, and a woman walks into the kitchen. She is wearing jeans and a white silk blouse, with blonde hair tied back in a loose knot. She has deep brown eyes. Alice hurries to embrace her.

This is Gabrielle, she says.

That was quick, I think, but do not say. The tent didn't even give me time to have a cup of coffee.

The newcomer greets me enthusiastically, taking my hand between both of hers and kissing me on both cheeks. I pull out a chair, so she is seated between Alice and myself.

Gabrielle is my friend and travelling companion, says Alice. Evidently she sees no need to engage in the social niceties that the arrival of a newcomer might normally involve. She takes it for granted that I will know Gabrielle has arrived *by tent*, as it were.

I, on the other hand, need more assurances.

Travelling companion? I say. Where are you going?

Oh, nowhere, Alice says. But in the past we travelled a fair bit together. And still do, occasionally.

Although, I add, you currently arrive at your destinations separately, and at different times, *if by means of the same vehicle*?

Alice smiles at me in saintly fashion, but says nothing.

The tent? I suggest, not wishing to let the subject go away so easily.

Ah yes, the tent, says Alice, trailing off into silence.

Well, I say, somewhat thrown by this lacuna: are we not going to talk about the tent?

My tent? says Gabrielle, with a convincing impression of innocence. Did you see it?

I did, I say. And a very fine tent it is too.

I prefer to not even consider the logistics of the thing: of how she pitched a tent – the same tent or a different one – in the space occupied by the tent that I vacated only minutes earlier.

Thank you, says Gabrielle. Your aunt, Megan, she gave it to me ...

Yes, I say. I kind of guessed ...

I am, at that moment, wondering how the tent manages its transformations, its shifts of affiliation. More specifically, I am wondering what has become of O'Hallaran's duffel bag and ethnic blanket. Although I saw them only minutes earlier, could they have already vanished, to be replaced by Gabrielle's belongings? Mumbling an excuse, I rush out into the garden and vault the fence into the field. The front flap of the tent has been left open. Inside, a dark green backpack lies across the groundsheet, a waterproof jacket slung over it. O'Hallaran's stuff is not there.

When I return to the kitchen I am still grinning.

Gabrielle lives in the Gers, in the south west of France. She and Alice have been close friends for some years: in fact, they were introduced by Megan, who had been best friends with Gabrielle's mother Zoë since their student days in Zurich ... Gabrielle explains herself with exemplary politeness, and her company is immeasurably preferable to O'Hallaran's. I am almost beside myself with self-congratulation on the success of my experiment.

From the Gers? Funny that, I say to Alice: wasn't that where O'Hallaran was living when he met Megan?

Alice nods, but does not seem particularly excited by the coincidence.

Although my family originally comes from the Gers, says Gabrielle, I have lived mostly in Paris. I have only recently moved back south.

And what brings you to Llys Rhosyn? I ask Gabrielle – not, of course, that I object to your visiting. Far from it; just curious, you know …

Oh, I knew Alice was here, says Gabrielle, and thought I would pay her a visit.

Really? I say, attempting to sound surprised. I turn to Alice: And you invited her along?

Alice nods, although she seems uncomfortable.

I have been here before, says Gabrielle, some years ago now. As Alice just said, my mother was a close friend of your aunt. I heard from her that Megan had died, and decided to visit the house while I was in Wales …

I don't know whether to believe this casual declaration – 'while I was in Wales' – but decide not to question her story, for now. The improvement in my mental state since emerging from the tent is most welcome. Since O'Hallaran's arrival I have been sunk into a kind of involuntary torpor, a pathetic state of doubt and self-pity, which climaxed the previous evening, when I drank too much, too quickly, fell over, and was spoken to by the fox. But now all that insecurity seems to have lifted. I reflect that it was just after Alice's mystery illness, with her as weak as a kitten, that O'Hallaran appeared and the change in me came about: Alice was miraculously cured, while I, by contrast, became weak, jealous and indecisive.

I was beginning to understand three things: (i) that on each occasion I emerged from the tent, a shift in the makeup and dynamic of the household took place; (ii) that whoever spilled forth from the tent was not necessarily going to provide a rational explanation for their own appearance, and should not be trusted to provide one, and (iii) that the tent and all who travelled in it were part of Megan's plan for me.

With regard to this last point, I was now convinced that my aunt's obscure intention, her secret legacy, was for me to interpret and resolve the challenges that the tent brought with it, replicating the challenge set by the library and its books, but with real human subjects: *One person opens another … compare them throughout and then you get the meaning. By reading one person alone you cannot get it, you cannot otherwise decipher it …*

I made my excuses and went to the library. I was sure Alice and her friend would have plenty to talk about.

That afternoon I work at my desk with the window open. I am studying an old manuscript, the *Aula Lucis* by Thomas Vaughan. I keep returning to a passage that demands my attention, no doubt because its reference to 'his glorious blue vestment' puts me in mind of the tent:

> *Hence you may gather some infallible signs, whereby you may direct yourselves in the knowledge of the Matter and in the operation itself, when the Matter is known. For if you have the true sperm and know withal how to prepare it – which cannot be without our secret fire – you shall find that the matter no sooner feels the philosophical heat but the white light will lift himself above the water, and there will he swim in his glorious blue vestment like the heavens.*

I glance up the drive, once again, just in case there is any sign of O'Hallaran, and at the same time wonder, vaguely, what the 'true sperm' might be, and whether I possess it, or indeed 'know withal how to prepare it'.

I can hear the voices of the two women, their laughter drifting in from the garden. This does not distract me at all: on the contrary, it pleases me, makes the place feel *lived in*. I open the window further and lean out. It is by now early evening, and there is the usual animated birdsong.

The women return inside. I close the window and leave the library to join them, choosing wine, a white Burgundy, and filling glasses from a jug of water, cool from the fridge. As there is a chill in the air, I suggest we eat inside tonight. I cannot help enacting the role of perfect host. I feel imbued with a new-found confidence, so distinct from my fretting, paranoid behaviour of the night before. I put a glass intended for Gabrielle in front of the fourth, free seat, then, in a triumphant moment, clear away O'Hallaran's place setting. As I do so, I experience a shudder of satisfaction.

The supper passes pleasantly enough: good food (cooked by Alice, with Gabrielle's help) and stimulating conversation. I don't wish to sound smug, but I am on rather good form myself. I feel calm and in control, as if recovered from a longstanding headache. I drink water and join in the talk, slipping in little stories from my travels, but do not hog the limelight, avoid doing that man thing in the company of two women, and I listen when listening seems the appropriate thing to do. However, I must admit to feeling somewhat apart, or disconnected, as though I am merely observing the actions of strangers. The usual sense of being dragged down by fatigue is entirely absent. I have forgotten my insomnia, or else have been magically refreshed by that brief sleep in the blue tent, or else – who knows – have reached a kind of plateau in my prolonged sleeplessness whereby everything that happens to me seems to be happening to another person, who carries on as though a simulacrum of myself, in my own skin and with my own voice, but from whom I am essentially detached.

It has been dark for some time when Alice says good night, and tells us she is going up to bed. If I think it odd that Gabrielle does not accompany her, I do not show it. But apparently Gabrielle does not wish to sleep; not yet, at least. A pot of mint tea that Alice has made before leaving sits on the table. Gabrielle pours. And as we sit there, the feeling of disconnection I have felt since emerging from the tent continues to mount in me.

Since I am experiencing a renewed sense of vigour, and am not remotely tired, it surprises me when Gabrielle remarks on how 'worn out' I look. I am almost affronted. Although I have indeed been exhausted for several weeks, I do not think it has become etched onto my face. Especially now, feeling rather spry. I deny that I am worn out, or even that I might look tired.

Yes, you do, she says, there is something about you, forgive me, a worn-out look, a tiredness that is not just of the surface. You remind me of someone I met, though only once. I hope I do not offend by telling you this. (No, no, I insist, go ahead, by all means – although to be honest, I am a little peeved.)

I was working, she says, at a bookshop on the left bank, the fifth arrondissement … and one day this guy came in, I thought he was probably in his twenties, but he looked older; rough, tired and sick. He had lost most of his hair and he wore a bandage around his neck, and he had protruding eyes. He was a young man *à l'allure de dandy*. I can say dandy? (You can say dandy, if you wish, I tell her.) He carried an elegant cane that came from another world, another century: the cane of a *flâneur*. It was black, with a silver handle. I was standing by the till. He tapped on the bookshop counter with this cane before he spoke, as though announcing himself by means of an instrument other than his voice, and he asked for *Les contes drolatiques de Balzac,* the request made, says Gabrielle, with a droll cynicism, an attention to the word 'drolatiques' that was most emphatic, to my mind indicating the kind of self-consciousness that I usually associate with writers, or would-be writers, or literary types in general. I have a lot to do with writers.

From a quick computer search, I learned that the book was out of print, so I told the guy *le livre est épuisé,* and then of course I felt awful because there is a double meaning to that word *épuisé,* since it means 'out of print' in relation to books but also exhausted, drained out, nothing left, which clearly might have sounded as though it were a direct commentary on the poor guy in front of me, that his life's book was empty, and I could feel his eyes on me and so I said something to fill the silence, that I knew the stories were frequently out in new collectors' editions, I mean it's Balzac after all, so I said to him, just in order to say something. 'They'll probably be reprinted some day.' The guy didn't seem to react at first, and then he said, with a sad or bitter smile, that he might be dead by then: *Mais je serai peut-être mort!* Jesus, what kind of a person says something like that to a shop assistant when they've just gone in to order a book? There was this conflict between what he was saying and the situation in which he was saying it, and with the two of us alone – well, not exactly alone, there was someone in the office and someone else in the storeroom, but we were alone in the front of the shop – I'm ashamed to admit it, but I was scared. It was as if he was in some way pleading with me, exposing me to all the hurt and outrage that he was suffering, and I felt *infected,* almost as though his despair was contagious, but, well, the relationship was still that of shop assistant and client, at least outwardly; and then he excused himself, his voice all croaky, and said he was dehydrated, and so I got him a glass of water. He drank it, thanked me, and then he left. And when he was gone I had the impression that for him, death waited at every corner, in every turning season, in every falling leaf.

When Gabrielle had finished speaking, she stirred her tea for a long time, to let the sugar soak in, and as she stirred she was staring at me, as if in a kind of trance.

So I said: And this guy reminded you of *me*? A dying man with a cane who came into your shop and drank a glass of water? I don't know what to say.

23

It is late by the time Gabrielle gets up to leave. I had assumed she would be sleeping in the house, in Alice's or else the spare room, but no, she seems set on sleeping in the tent. She asks if I will walk with her 'down the garden path', yes, she uses that expression – whether knowing its colloquial significance or not – which amuses me then, but not as much as it will later. She takes my arm and draws close, much closer than is necessary, certainly more than seems strictly appropriate. When we reach the little gate that leads into the field she leans forward and kisses me, slipping her tongue between my lips, between my teeth, at first gently, then probing deeper. Her thighs press tight against mine. Her breath is hot on my face and she smells sweet and musty.

She leads me by the hand and we duck beneath the flysheet, into the tent's nest, and she undresses, first me and then herself. Gabrielle operates with a skilled determination. She is supple and needy, and any residual fatigue I may have been enduring from my sleepless nights is banished as she sits astride me and shakes loose her long blonde hair, which falls about my face. She leans over me and with her mouth on mine she kisses me deeply, then sucks at my tongue, a most bizarre, but agreeable sensation, while below she manoeuvres me inside her. Then she sits up straight, takes my hands and places them on her breasts, my palms flat on her hard nipples, and her movements and gyrations, slow at first, begin to accelerate, provoking us both into an excited – and she into an exuberantly noisy – state of sustained bliss. After such a long period of sexual abstinence, my body's mass release of endorphins is overwhelming and I ejaculate, just as she, with laudable timing, pauses in mid-motion, arches her back, and lets out a protracted cry.

It is a most convincing performance. I don't mean that as a slur on Gabrielle, far from it; more as a reflection that despite the intense pleasure I derive from our coupling, it doesn't seem to be happening to me, or even to *us*, but rather to two actors whom I am observing from afar.

I pull away from under her and fling myself onto my side. The air in the tent is stifling and I pull up the zip, to let the night in. Gabrielle has settled to sleep, flat out after her exertions, and I try to make myself comfortable, which is difficult in the confines of the tent. I drift on the edges of slumber for a half hour or so, the events of the day and its unexpected climax playing out on repeat, with only a dim awareness of Gabrielle's warm and sleeping body by my side. Even when the afterglow has dissipated, I feel more alive than I have for a long time. But I know I must leave: if by some miracle I were to sleep, I do not want to wake up in the tent. Or rather, I don't want to be seen emerging from it, and certainly not by Alice.

So I get dressed, finding my clothes with difficulty in the dark, and return to the house, to the library, and I prepare a fire, or rather I build on the ashes of the fire that has nearly died. I select newspaper and kindling, setting about the task meticulously. Once the logs are ablaze, I am about to get up, when I see a book lying on the edge of the rug, a book I have not, until this moment, noticed lying there, nor – I am certain of this – have I removed it from the shelves myself. It has been left open on a poem entitled 'Art of War'. I read the poem aloud:

A rose at the window has the colours
of a blonde's young nipple
a mole walks underground.
Peace they say to the dog
whose life is short.
The air remains sunlit.
Young men learn to make war
in order to redeem a whole world
so they are told
but to them the book of theory
remains unreadable.

I read the poem as though it bore a direct relevance to my own predicament, my own life, even hoping that it might contain some clue or message, beyond the rather obvious reference to the 'blonde' at the beginning. I do this simply because the book is there, open at this page, so I deduce, in a not unreasonable way, that it has been left out for me. I am particularly struck by the idea that, for the young men, the book of theory remains unreadable. What else have I been doing in the library this past year, other than studying books of theory instead of living a life? But making war? How is that pertinent to me? And why am I assuming that the poem has *something to tell me*? I put the book down. I guess that Alice must have been in the library. Perhaps she came here after supper, when she left the kitchen, rather than retiring to bed, picked out a book at random and neglected to return it to its shelf …

I am not sure how long I have been seated on the rug – caught between reflection on my recent *liaison* with Gabrielle and the poem I am studying – when I am alerted by a scratching sound from outside: a grating, or scraping of something heavy against concrete.

I cannot quite identify the sound, but I know its source is not too distant, and that it emanates from the kitchen garden, or perhaps a little further away, towards the woods. I step out through the French windows onto the patio. It is cold, and there is damp in the air. Despite an almost full moon and a clear sky, the night has taken an inhospitable turn and a wind is stirring, causing the branches of trees and bushes to rustle and sway. I set off in the direction from which the noise originated. To one side of the kitchen garden is an old woodshed, where logs and a few gardening tools are kept, and it is toward this shed that my footsteps lead me. I push open the heavy wooden door and as it drags against the concrete, I recognise the grating sound that alerted me at my desk. Inside, I can see nothing at first. But someone is groaning at the far end of the shed, and I hear their laboured breath. Stepping forward, moonlight floods in from the open doorway behind me. Huddled in the corner is a human shape, draped, it would appear, in a rug or covering of some kind; and I make out – as I knew, a split-second beforehand, that I would – O'Hallaran's face, haggard in the dim light.

I step closer, intrigued. I am close enough now to see that his face is bloodied and bruised: he looks as though he has taken a beating. Human sympathy takes over from curiosity and I stand over him, intending to ask him what is the matter. But he cowers from me, pulling his covering close – it turns out to be his ethnic blanket – as though this will somehow offer him protection. I crouch, so that we are at a level, and to help assure him that I mean no harm.

What happened to you? I ask, and reach out a hand, meaning to grasp his shoulder in a supportive gesture. Again, he draws back from me.

Don't be afraid, I say. I'm not going to hurt you.

He is shaking. I notice his duffle bag at his side. He is not a person I would have associated with this state of abject fear. O'Hallaran, with his ready wit, was a man with a quip for all occasions; but not now, as I squat beside him in this uneasy silence.

Can I get you something? I ask, finally. Do you want water, a hot drink? Whisky?

I am thinking that his face could do with a good clean. That wound above the eye looks nasty, and might need stitches.

He shakes his head and waves both hands at me in a violent gesture, as though shooing away a dog, while shuffling back, retreating towards the wall of the shed. He pulls the blanket tight around him.

I try one last time, in an offer of unprecedented generosity:

Would you like to sleep inside the house? There is a spare bed. It'll be warmer there. You'll be more comfortable. Or would you like to tell Alice what has happened, someone else, rather than me?

Just Fuck Off, he cries out finally, hoarsely, shaking his head, tears smearing his cheeks: *For fuck's sake leave me alone. Leave me here. I cannot, will not move. I will wash me fucking face in the morning. Now sod off and leave me be.*

I remain crouched at his side, pondering this outburst. Does he even recognise me? Is he drunk? I did catch the whiff of alcohol on him … but he has given no real sign of recognition, merely treated me as though I were one amongst a host of terrors, another phantom come to torment him. What can have happened to O'Hallaran to reduce him to this pathetic state?

There is no point in trying to bring about a rescue when the object of my goodwill so evidently wishes to be left alone. I stand slowly and retreat to the door, and O'Hallaran remains huddled against the far wall, as if unable to bear my presence. As I close the door behind me, it makes the same ominous scraping sound that led me here. I need to clear my head, again. I need to think.

Returning to the kitchen I make tea – builder's tea, with sugar – and retire to the library. I draw the armchair closer to the fire, and pull my feet up beneath me.

I have rarely witnessed so thorough a transformation as has come over O'Hallaran. And all of this since my entering the blue tent this morning. Am I, therefore, in some way responsible for what has happened to him? Was his distress caused by whatever physical injury was done to him, exacerbated by a more ominous and general sense of terror? Or was it on account of seeing me? Which was why I suggested bringing Alice to him, knowing that he was fond of her, which in turn proves I did not loathe O'Hallaran quite as much as I had made out to myself that I did, even if – to be honest – his return was most unwelcome. Whatever the cause of his misery, I was not going to force him to talk, or drag him down to the house against his will. In spite of his anguish, he seemed resigned to his own woeful condition. This, bizarrely, struck me as an attitude for which the tent itself was somehow responsible. I remembered the way that Alice had accepted O'Hallaran's claim to ownership of the tent without any obvious concern; she had treated it almost as a matter of course and had reacted to her own ousting in a manner which, at the time, had seemed absurdly passive.

Outside, the night is edging into day, and an impressively punctual cockerel starts up from the direction of Morgan's farm. I put another log on the fire and settle into my armchair. My thoughts return to O'Hallaran. Perhaps I shouldn't be too concerned: he could always wander over to the house if he feels the need for human company. I will not begrudge him the warmth of my hearth and a cup of coffee. Perhaps Alice will reproach me for not having told her immediately about

O'Hallaran's injury. On the other hand, would it be entirely absurd to suspect that Alice already knows about O'Hallaran's return? She seems to be abreast of pretty much everything else that goes on around the house. The day before, she certainly seemed to be expecting Gabrielle – more precisely, she had *arranged* it. Which brings me to thinking about Gabrielle, and the brief encounter that marked the start of the night's adventures. How spontaneous was it, on Gabrielle's part? How much of a coincidence was it that Alice should bid us goodnight and go to bed early, giving Gabrielle and myself time to get better acquainted? Especially now that I know she did not go straight up to bed, but was in the library, where I must assume she was reading poetry even as Gabrielle and I were fucking in the blue tent.

Was Alice a party to Gabrielle's seduction of me? And if so, why? And the poem – if it was intended for me, and I can think of no other reason why the book would be left open on the rug – what relation if any, does it bear on the events of the night? Or, on the contrary, was my fifteen minutes of passion with the Frenchwoman something I should conceal from Alice; would it inspire jealousy and cause offence – even if it was not, exactly, at my instigation?

Tired now, but knowing I will not be able to sleep, and still bubbling with the febrile energy of the night, I wander over to the window. As I stand there, the fox trots by, at a distance of only a few yards, returning from his nocturnal scavenging. I have not seen him since he spoke to me, or I imagined him speaking to me. I smile, as one does at the sight of animals going about their business, oblivious to human society – inhabitants of a world that is contiguous with our own, and yet separate – and he stops dead, one forepaw raised in a characteristic gesture, before taking off again at a run, and climbing to the upper lawn, where the woods begin.

24

By now other birds, songsters of the middle air, have joined the yokel cockerel in celebrating the advance of daylight. I decide to go and wake Alice, and tell her of the wounded man in the woodshed. She is sprawled across her double bed, stirs reluctantly and then, when she sees me, sits up, rubs her eyes, and hugs me warmly. This display of affection takes me by surprise, and I am moved, more than just a little.

I tell her that I heard a noise during the night, coming from the woodshed, and went to investigate. I tell her the state in which I found O'Hallaran, battered and bloody. She looks concerned – but doesn't appear to find the news entirely unexpected, is not entirely shocked or surprised, nor does she ask me why I didn't tell her earlier. She gets up, wrapping the throw around herself, and asks me to wait while she showers. When she returns – dressed for a summer's day in trainers, shorts and a T-shirt – we set off into the garden, and up towards the woodshed.

As we approach, I feel unduly nervous. Recent events at Llys Rhosyn are tinged with a sense of unreality, and I am even beginning to wonder whether I imagined some of last night's unfoldings. Alice strides along beside me, seemingly at ease with the world, Keto the dog bouncing at her heels. We march to the accompaniment of trilling birdsong.

At the woodshed, I push the door open, with the now familiar, grating response. The interior is revealed in far greater clarity than it was during my night visit. The logs are piled neatly in rows to our left and, to the right, long-handled gardening shears, a hoe, an axe, a spade, a fork, an upturned wheelbarrow; all are carefully arranged, the legacy of Aunt Megan's reign as custodian of garden tools, and one which O'Hallaran and Alice are now continuing. I also spot some boxes of shrubs and a few sacks whose contents I have never explored …

But at the far end of the shed, where last night he lay cowering, there is no sign of O'Hallaran, although his duffle bag and blanket mark the spot, testimony to his presence, and likely return. Keto sniffs at them, and looks up at us expectantly, tail thrashing.

I stand there feeling foolish, a slow-witted detective.

Well, he's not here now, I say.

Alice looks around the shed and kicks up a little dust. There on the floor, leading from his sleeping place to the door, is an irregular trail of what appears to be blood. We search in vain for any other signs of O'Hallaran's passage. Outside again, we are met by the sun rising over the valley, with Llys Rhosyn to our left, and there on the edge of Morgan's field, straight ahead, the blue tent is a solitary artefact, source of all that has come to pass.

Let's go wake Gabrielle, says Alice.

Right, I say, a little hesitantly. Let's do that.

It only takes a minute to cross the garden and reach the tent. Alice stands outside and calls her friend's name. There is no answer. She bends and unzips the entrance. I decide I do not wish to be immediately visible.

But inside – just as at the woodshed – there is only the minimal evidence of occupancy; Gabrielle's sleeping bag, and a small backpack. Their owner – the tent's current occupant – has already left. I turn and take in the landscape. Crows are circling the tops of the beech trees high in the woods, making a terrible racket. Clouds are scudding fast over the mountains to the west. And across Morgan's field, from the direction of the stream, Alice and I both spot O'Hallaran coming towards us, his slow, easy gait unimpeded by any obvious injury. As he gets closer, I call out a greeting, which he returns with a cheerful wave. Alice starts walking towards him, and I follow.

Glad to see you looking so much better, I say, when we are within speaking distance.

O'Hallaran is inclined, it would seem, to put last night's encounter behind him. Aw, he says, I stopped off for a couple of pints in the village (he doesn't say which village) and rather forgot myself on the way home. Took a tumble.

Forgot himself? Took a tumble? He is obviously lying. But why? Why should he need to lie, and what is he concealing?

He has been down at the stream at the far end of Morgan's field, he says. To freshen up. Fair play to him: he never asks to use the bathroom in the house, and this is why. He comes to the stream – which hereabouts is quite wide, and could be considered a small river – and carries out his ablutions like a true frontiersman, in a pool deep enough to stand in up to the chest. I peer at him carefully while attempting not to make it obvious that I am inspecting his face for the wound I noticed the night before. There is a deep graze above the eyebrow on the left side. It still looks like it might need stitches, but has been thoroughly washed. There is colourful bruising around the eye itself.

O'Hallaran knows I am examining his face, and puts up with it. Then, as if to break the tension – Alice, thus far, has uttered not a word – he drops his shoulder bag to the ground and pulls out two medium-sized trout. Breakfast, he says. They were just lounging around in the pool, lazy feckers. So I tickled them out.

I am impressed. Truly, O'Hallaran has earned his wild man spurs. Alice gazes at the fish. Wow, she says. I have never met anyone who could do that. She squats and turns one over in her hand. A good weight too, she adds.

133

O'Hallaran shrugs modestly, and strokes his beard.

Why has O'Hallaran made no mention of the blue tent's new tenant? He obviously knows someone is there. For one thing, his own belongings must have been removed and placed elsewhere, either by him, or by Gabrielle. Is he adopting the same nonchalance that Alice did when, on his own arrival at Llys Rhosyn, the tent suddenly became *his* – despite its previous affiliation to her? Has he, after all these years as its owner, now been *dumped* by the tent? The thought almost makes me feel sorry for him. Perhaps this was partly why he was so upset the night before ... apart from the crack on the head, of course.

I am distracted from these thoughts by Alice tugging at my sleeve. Look, she says, and points down the drive. Gabrielle is approaching from the direction of the road, riding an old-fashioned lady's bicycle that I have previously noticed in the lean-to near the back door, once used for storing coal. A bicycle neither I nor Alice (nor O'Hallaran) had thought of trying out, but which Gabrielle has discovered and appropriated. As she reaches the end of the drive she alights – most elegantly, I observe, with a delicate sashay – pushing the bike for the few remaining yards towards the kitchen door.

Alice and I climb back across the field to the garden, intending to join Gabrielle inside. As we turn to enter the kitchen, O'Hallaran mutters quickly, I won't be joining you just now ... have things to do ... here, take the fish. And he passes the two trout to Alice, and hurries off up towards the woodshed. He seems in a terrible hurry.

25

I set about grilling the trout for breakfast, and Gabrielle helps in the kitchen, preparing a fruit salad. She doesn't ask where the fish have come from, but in answer to a question from Alice, I let slip O'Hallaran's name, and immediately Gabrielle appears uneasy. I feel certain that there is bad blood between the two of them. I am curious to know whether, if this is the case, the source of their antagonism is based on a disputed tenancy of the tent, or whether they knew each other before coming to the house. But I do not ask.

O'Hallaran does not make an appearance at breakfast.

Gabrielle's attitude towards me is affectionate but discreet. She is fond of making physical contact, her hand on my arm or shoulder when we speak, but no one observing us would have guessed that only the evening before we enjoyed an encounter of uninhibited passion.

After our late breakfast, as the three of us are cleaning up the kitchen, Alice says she wants to work in the greenhouse, and suggests I take Gabrielle for a walk. She likes the outdoor life, you know, says Alice. Hiking up mountains, all that stuff. And she knows the names of all the birds, don't you, Gabi …

I am not sure quite what Alice is playing at, but I am not going along with it. I could no more leave the grounds of Llys Rhosyn right now than cut off my right hand. I cannot even bring myself to go shopping for food, and I make a mental note to order a delivery from the supermarket.

I tell Alice that if I want to know the names of all the birds I can google them, and I leave for the library.

This little outburst surprises me as much as it does Alice, but I feel that I am being played, and I don't like it.

In the library, I settle to a study by a seventeenth-century Dutch scholar, Pietr van Nootebaum entitled (in its translation from the Latin) *A most Fortunate and Timely Exegesis of the Kabbalistic Wisdom of the Aleph*, but I find it hard to concentrate. It occurs to me that Alice wanted Gabrielle and me out of the way so that she could speak with O'Hallaran without fear of interruption. But she could have managed that without us having to leave the house altogether. I cannot understand what she is trying to engineer.

My rumination is cut short by a knock on the door. It is Gabrielle, carrying a tray on which stand a pot of coffee and two cups. She looks about, assessing her surroundings – I assume it is the first time she has been inside the library, and then remember she has visited the house before, with her mother – and she asks if I am busy, but not in a way that seriously suggests I might be, or that if I were it would deter her.

I gesture to her to put the tray down on a small table alongside the green armchair. She pours the coffee and brings me a cup, settling herself on a hard-backed chair that she places alongside the desk, next to my own. She sits on the chair backwards, as it were, like a cowboy in a Western, legs apart. I am a little uneasy about her close proximity. There is certainly a *frisson* between us. However, I find it difficult – although not, if I am entirely honest, impossible – to consider exploring a longer-term sexual relationship. Fortunately, Gabrielle doesn't expect me to investigate this dilemma with her. Instead – most conveniently, in the light of my own unanswered questions – she starts asking about O'Hallaran.

How long, she says, have you known this man O'Hallaran, who is staying at your house? The one I saw this morning, who brought the fish.

Not long, I reply. Three weeks or so. And he isn't exactly staying in my house. He seems to have decided on squatting in the woodshed.

Squatting?

Living as an unofficial resident, or non-paying tenant. Why do you ask?

He is not such a good person, I think.

Why? I ask. What has O'Hallaran done?

Last night, after you left … I was half asleep and I heard sounds outside, someone moving around, bumping into the side of the tent. I knew it wasn't you. Then the zip was pulled down. Obviously I thought it was an intruder …

It was O'Hallaran?

Yes, it was, she says, quietly.

That is not so surprising, you know. He will have thought he was coming home to his tent.

His tent?

O'Hallaran mistook your tent for his own, since he possesses a blue tent also. Possibly the very one that you own, although I cannot go into that now; it's complicated. But you, presumably, took fright, took offence …

Gabrielle is looking down at the ground, shaking her head. She begins to mutter something in French, and then she looks up – I'm afraid I did rather more than take offence, she says, in answer to my remark. I pushed him backwards and hit him with a baseball bat.

Jesus, I say.

Well, I travel with a baseball bat, she explains. I started playing in Montréal.

Oh well, I say, as if that explained everything. It must come in useful when the special protection of the tent doesn't prove sufficient.

Exactly, she says, oblivious to my sarcasm.

Please, I ask her, after pausing to digest her confession: tell me about the tent.

What do you mean? What do you want to know? she asks.

How did you acquire the tent, Gabrielle? You say it was a gift from my Aunt Megan, but what was the occasion of her giving it to you?

Megan gave me the tent six or seven years ago, when I was visiting Llys Rhosyn. It was just after my twenty-first birthday. She said that since I had begun to travel, I was going to need a special tent, that might, if I looked after it, offer me a degree of protection.

What did you make of her saying that? I mean, did that not sound odd to you?

Well, it might have, if I hadn't been brought up listening to all kinds of stuff of a similar kind. From my mother as well as Megan. They were both – despite being scientists – also susceptible to some very strange ideas. Well, strange to most people anyway. About alchemy, synchronicity, the transcendent properties of objects, and so on. It was the early influence of Jung, and MLF, you know …

MLF?

Marie-Louise von Franz, their teacher or mentor. I thought you knew all this.

I do, some of it, I say, evasive.

She looks at me curiously for a moment, but does not continue.

Last night, I begin, deciding that I might as well clear the air … when we had sex in the tent …

She interrupts me, gentle, but assertive: Listen, she says … you mustn't trust what happens inside the tent. I don't know what you remember, and whether it's the same as I remember, but you cannot take as reality whatever happens to you inside the tent. I mean, you cannot treat it in the same way as what happens in the world outside.

What are you saying? Are you saying we didn't … that what went on between us didn't happen?

I'm not saying it *didn't*, she says. But within the context of the blue tent, it doesn't mean it *did* happen either. Can you understand that?

Oh, I say. Well, no. Not really.

But while I did not understand it, I thought I could just about imagine the paradox she was suggesting: that within the tent itself, things could both happen and not happen. I had already felt a hint of how that might be possible, on my previous visits to the tent, because of the tenuous and implausible nature of my experiences within it, the powerful sense of occupying a separate reality. It was as if the tent offered a distinct or parallel version of events. The phrase 'a dubious textile' suddenly drops into consciousness, blown there from who knows where …

26

Later that afternoon, when I go to the kitchen in search of something to eat, Gabrielle tells me she has spoken with O'Hallaran, and apologised for banging him on the head with a baseball bat. She says that he has accepted her apology, along with her invitation to have the tent back. She then asks me if she can move in with Alice. I reply that she could do better than that: there are at least three other bedrooms, and she is welcome to any one of them. She says that it is kind of me to offer, but that she and Alice are old friends and more than happy to share a room. The bed, she says, is big enough for the two of us. For three even, she adds, deadpan.

I also manage to track down Alice, who is taking a break from tending to her potted plants, and ask her why – since they had been in touch, and for all I knew had spoken via some phone App – she hadn't warned Gabrielle about O'Hallaran's occupation of the blue tent *before* she arrived at Llys Rhosyn. Alice merely shrugs and says I didn't think to. It hadn't been a problem for me when O'Hallaran turned up, so I didn't think to. To my mind, that sounds a bit suspect. Sometimes Alice's fecklessness bewilders me, if that's what it is.

I watch Gabrielle and O'Hallaran through the kitchen window, as I make myself a sandwich. They are out by the greenhouse, examining the bicycle that Gabrielle was riding earlier in the day. If his body language is anything to go by, O'Hallaran still seems to be slightly wary of her, but that is hardly surprising.

That evening I venture upstairs for a change of clothes.

Through the window of my bedroom I am able to watch Gabrielle pulling a rucksack from the tent with one hand, a baseball bat in the other. Alice trails alongside her, carrying a sleeping bag and a pair of hiking shoes.

As I had already deduced, all the changes that had come about since Alice first arrived – including her initial appearance in my kitchen – were brought about by some specific action of my own. I had started all this, and somehow *invoked* Alice, magically rendering her present. The same was true of the others: I had gone inside the tent, and some time later O'Hallaran and Gabrielle had appeared, by turn, and claimed to have arrived with the tent. Every development had been dependent upon me taking action, specifically by my going inside the tent. Perhaps the tent had arrived before any of its occupants, unaccompanied. Who could tell? But every development affirmed, in some way, a direct link with my Aunt Megan, and to Llys Rhosyn itself. It had become clear to me that my own decisive action was all that was required, and rather than watching and waiting, in order to see what might happen now that it was temporarily vacant – awaiting O'Hallaran's return – I should step inside the tent immediately, and attempt to incite or invoke the next stage or phase.

I hear the two women come up the stairs and into Alice's bedroom. They are talking and laughing, bound up in private matters, secrets, little jokes, who knows what. I listen at the door, and hear my own name. I am not surprised at this, but once I have heard what I suspected I would hear – on a subject both scurrilous and arousing – I cannot bring myself to eavesdrop any longer, and set off down the stairs quietly, out through the rose garden, and stand next to the blue tent. I can see Alice's bedroom window from where I stand, but there is no figure silhouetted there, as mine had been at the window next to it a few minutes earlier, only the clouds reflected from a constipated sky.

The entrance flap has been left open.

Once inside, the tent seems to have taken on a slightly weary or ironic aspect since I first saw it pitched there in pristine May sunshine. It almost seems a parody of its former self, but I am sure this idea of the tent's obsolescence is of my own making, that I am projecting my own emotional fatigue onto a mere length of cloth, a piece of textile.

Nevertheless, this time it feels different. I turn to zip up the entrance behind me, and can sense the change, and also a certain danger. The blueness is less intense, less all-consuming. It is as if the blue has lost some of that energy, which has been superseded by a more insidious element, or colour, or emotion; more grey than blue, more alien, corrupt, synthetic.

I do not swoon as I did when I first came into the tent all that time ago, when everything was a sweep of overwhelming blue. But I know the white-streaked greyness that has replaced it represents a transitional state, and as I lie on the floor of the tent, the grey descends in tone towards a deeper substantiality; a spongy volcanic rockiness with the reek of burning, a residue of scorched metal, of *materiel* incinerated in the aftermath of battle, the abandoned husks of tanks and armoured cars. I know that this is the state to which everything will eventually be reduced, and although I do not know how exactly that will come about, I somehow *remember* it: young men learn to make war in order to redeem the world. A deep red suffuses the tent and seeps through the grey mist of burning steel.

A wheezy accordion attempts to play me to sleep, but here I do not or cannot sleep, am alert and hostile, waiting for the tent to take off, fly away, a device that feeds off time like a vulture on a dead dog, whose life is short, the one I saw at the roadside once ... where was it now? ... and there were distant poplars ...

The tent grows and is a massive dance hall beside a lake, someone says in voiceover *1945* and there is an orchestra playing as the dance hall fills with couples jitterbugging. A young girl, who I recognise as Megan, looks on in confusion as, with a whirr and flapping of wings, a host of water birds, pink flamingos, alight on the lake, then sink into thick black oil ... There is a beating of wind on the side of the tent. The voice that said *1945* now says *After love all animals are sad* ... The dance hall fades and I am at a roadside in a barren, windswept landscape. *Peace they say* and again I stand before my Aunt Megan, the brightly hued bolts of textile spread on the ground before her as she looks down upon a pit containing a huge pile of bones; *This was my generation*, she says without emotion, the Cold War generation, *we embarked on solitary crusades into darkness*; and then she leaves and I am alone in the tent, and I hear the same voice as before say *First the text and then the textile*, and I am alone and lost on a winding path, nearing the end of my journey, poplars at the wayside; *Peace they say*, and I have no memory of what came before, or of how I came to be in this place ...

Confusingly, the sound of O'Hallaran's voice replaces that of my dream's invisible narrator.

Bejaysus, he says, sounding like a stage Paddy, – you never know who you're going to find inside the fuckin' thing. Last time I paid a visit to me own tent some demented harpy attacks me with a crowbar; now the master of the house himself is found having a kip within.

I sit up, rudely awakened by this outburst. O'Hallaran's face, illuminated by a torch he holds, glowers at me ruddily in the entrance to the tent. He has evidently bathed again, and his hair, still wet, is brushed straight back from the forehead.

He has trimmed his beard, and looks younger, is fresher-faced, as though he has applied some kind of unguent or moisturiser. In the ghostly light of the torch, despite the impressive bruising around one of them, his eyes appear very blue, as though he were wearing tinted lenses. I surely must have noticed this before. As blue as the tent ever was. His lips are blood-red. He has definitely been a lady's man in his day, I would venture, oh most definitely. And he is transformed on the inside too; compared with the terrified creature I met in the woodshed, his manner and mood are unrecognisable.

I break off from these reflections on O'Hallaran's physical charms and mental state, and fully emerge from my trance, or however I might describe the state into which the tent has sent me.

Good morning, I say. Or is it?

After midnight, he says, as the song goes.

Well, I have had a good rest then, I lie. The tent does that for me, at least. You'll be wanting it back, as I gather from the intro.

The woodshed has its pleasures, he says, but they are few and of a basic, hard-arsed nature.

Rustic, I add.

Quite so. And you, after all, the owner of a great pile like Llys Rhosyn, hardly need a wigwam too. Tell me, he adds, this isn't the first time you've slept inside the tent, is it?

No, I say. This is, let me see, my fourth visit. And on every occasion I have slept, after a fashion. Which for me is a luxury in itself.

He looks pensive. He fiddles with his newly-trimmed moustache.

So, he says, you visited my tent before I arrived here, if that is possible?

I did, I reply. And it is.

144

O'Hallaran shakes his head, a little sadly. Is he sad because he has discovered that he is not the unique owner – or even tenant – of the tent, or because his existence as the easy-going resident vagabond at Llys Rhosyn has been shattered by Gabrielle's assault on him the night before?

Tell me, he says, – what was it like when you first went inside the tent, without any knowledge of its, shall we say … its charms or special properties?

Very blue, I say. Blue in the extreme. It felt like entering a world of blue.

And now?

Now, I muse, half in answer to his question and half in response to my own; now it seems like a place of tumult if not of desolation … but what am I saying, telling you, of all people, of the tent's capacity for transformation? I'm sorry, I add, if I sound pompous.

Oh, that is of no concern, says O'Hallaran. Be as pompous as the Pope for all I care. I am still curious about the tent, you see, even after all these years. Around thirty, give or take. It is a most unusual apparatus, the blue tent, what with the different effects it has on people … With me, nowadays, I hardly feel much at all, compared, say, to the early years. Apart from the occasional sadness. But in you, it would seem, the tent has found a perfect conduit. Now why would that be, do you think?

Well, I say, I haven't thought about it much.

Hmm, says O'Hallaran. He appears unconvinced, but I am disinclined to share with him any further thoughts I might have on the topic of the tent.

Well, I say, you'll be wanting it back, your tent, at any rate. So I had better leave.

If you would be so kind, says O'Hallaran, I would then be able to get some decent shut-eye.

O'Hallaran moves aside, so I can crawl out of the tent. Once I am outside I too stand. A bright, cool night. There is a full moon now, and the stars form a tapestry of jewels. An owl hoots from the wood. I remember Alice, and feel an odd shiver of anticipation, or something else, tinged with a kind of fear … and yet I feel benign towards O'Hallaran, and put my arm around his shoulder.

That is one hell of a whack Gabrielle gave you, I say.

Aye, he rubs his forehead above the bruised eye. The girl gave me no time to explain myself, no time at all.

And he disengages from me, crouches, kneels, and enters the tent.

27

Back in the library, I am wide awake, and I re-read the poem I discovered on the rug the night before. I try to make sense of it in relation to the message left for me, long ago, by Megan. *One book opens the other …*

Every book might lead to another, and every text might be replicated in cloth or textile. I am beginning to think the tent is the textual repository of the entire library. The book of theory, perhaps. But I have also been reminded, by my tryst with Gabrielle, of another texture, that of the flesh. And there is a new element, which I can trace to the moment I left the blue tent on this last occasion: there are string quartets playing in my head. The music came in snatches at first, but now is almost continuous.

Shortly before four in the morning the door opens and Alice steps into the library. At first I think she is sleepwalking; her step is unsteady, her gaze unfocused. Did she leave her own bed while still asleep? Does she awaken at the same time every night, and set off downstairs to the library in a semi-conscious state, only realising where she is when she arrives at the threshold of the library? Whatever the case, she seems to recognise me of a sudden – having been inside the library for a full ten seconds – and she smiles. But the delay in this moment of recognition strikes me as strange. It makes me think, absurd though the notion is – that perhaps I am only partially visible, or else that I am visible only some of the time. Or else Alice herself is not entirely present. Why did she not greet me from the doorway? Is it because she is not truly there, or is it because she cannot always see me?

I must not think like this. She sees me, of course she sees me. I may be an insomniac, with string quartets playing in my head, but I am not a ghost, not a phantom spirit.

Hullo, she says. I didn't see you there, for a minute. A trick of the light.

The pyjamas are not part of the agenda tonight. Instead she is wearing a pale blue shirt, a man's shirt – which I recognise as my own, borrowed from my bedroom, no doubt.

She approaches and slides onto the rug in front of the fireplace, adopting her usual cross-legged pose.

I saw you go inside the tent, she says, after a long while.

You did?

Yes, she says. I was in your room. Peeping from behind the curtain.

Oh. Why did you go into my room?

I wanted to borrow a shirt. And to see if you had any nice ties, she says.

And did you find any?

No, she says, I was disappointed.

There is a long silence. I know that this is not the only occasion she has been through my stuff, ransacked my bedroom – before hastily restoring it to a semblance of its former state – in a search that seemed inspired by a far more powerful motive than the mere quest for a tie, or any other such article.

I reflect on her last response, and the nature of her disappointment, before conjuring my next question. But Alice beats me to it, catching me off guard:

How did you enjoy Gabrielle's thighs? she says. In the tent. Last night.

Delay would be disastrous, but I have no ready answer to this question.

I didn't, I say.

Oh, she says. That's not what Gabrielle says. She says, and I quote, minus the cute accent, that you 'fucked her brains out'.

O Lord, I say. I never did. She's lying.

I may as well deny it, especially as Gabrielle has told me that what happens inside the tent hasn't necessarily taken place in reality; and besides – I think, but do not say – that during the act of coitus Gabrielle was on top, so who, technically speaking, fucked whom?

Now, why would she do that? says Alice. Why would Gabrielle lie to me?

God knows. To make you jealous?

Do I seem jealous?

I look at her.

No, I say.

Quite, she says. What's a fuck between friends?

I ask myself: does Gabrielle qualify as a 'friend' on the first day I meet her? Or is Alice referring to the friendship between Gabrielle and herself? Is my fucking of, or being fucked by Gabrielle mediated in some way by her pre-existing friendship with Alice? Am I missing something?

So? she says, with an upward intonation that suggests it is my turn to provide further detail.

So? What do you mean? So nothing. So I didn't fuck her. I mean, not *exactly*. Would you prefer it if I had? Is that what you two were nattering about on the stairs, when you moved her stuff into your room?

Is that what we women do, natter?

On this occasion, yes, natter seems an apposite verb. You and your friend were discussing your sexual preferences in an informal fashion, and I happened to overhear.

There is again a long pause and, as I seem to remember happening once before, I hear sounds that I cannot reasonably

149

be hearing: the scratching of a mole beneath the soil on the back lawn; the dew forming on the grass outside my window … Perhaps I am going insane.

We are here for your own good, you know, she says. You don't realise how lucky you are. You should appreciate it.

And springing to her feet, she crosses the library floor with a sprightly step, offering no valediction as she closes the door behind her. Seconds later I hear the patter of her feet on the floor above. There is the sound of voices, and of laughter, and a cold wave of uncertainty washes over me.

28

The string quartets in my head have become a permanent feature now, and although the music is fluent and flawless – reminiscent at times of Beethoven's final works – I do not, on the whole, consider this development to be a good thing. For the past few days it has been a more or less continuous performance. I mention it to Alice, and she simply says 'lucky you', which kind of misses the point. In my desperation for sleep – and to somehow muffle the string quartets; to quell some of the more frantic movements, if not banish them entirely – I have taken a generous helping of sleeping pills on a couple of occasions, but these barely scratch the surface, and the music plays on. My thinking has become more erratic and I am prone to long periods of staring into the middle distance.

It is the third evening since I went inside the tent. Life at Llys Rhosyn has again settled into a kind of routine, with O'Hallaran and Alice working in the garden or the greenhouse during the day, Gabrielle busying herself in the kitchen or stretched out on the sofa in the sitting room, reading, and me toiling away at my desk in the library for hours on end, engaged in lacklustre, and increasingly disenchanted 'literary research', as I call it. I am waiting for something to happen following my fourth visit to the tent, because something always does happen but thus far, after more than forty-eight hours, there have been no new developments. Compare that with the fact that Alice showed up within half an hour of my first going inside the tent, and O'Hallaran appeared almost immediately after I ventured in the second time. With Gabrielle, we only had to wait a matter of minutes. The lapse between my entering the tent and someone turning up at the house has been diminishing, not growing. So this is an anomaly. Maybe the tent needs time to make up its mind. Maybe it has decided that this is the total sum of persons it has at its disposal – all three of them having acquired tents (or *a* tent, at least) from Aunt Megan. Maybe the tent has had its say and this is what it is going to be like from now on, with myself and Alice as friends and sparring partners, my relationship with Gabrielle shrouded in ambiguity and – on my part, at least – a hearty dose of lust; Alice and Gabrielle as room-mates, and Gabrielle and O'Hallaran polite and outwardly friendly, but still mutually suspicious of each other. A pretty standard kind of set-up within a dysfunctional family, no? The dog, Keto, has made himself very much a part of the place, and is the only member of the household unaffected by any of the fluctuating sympathies between the others in our little community.

I have taken to spending more time with O'Hallaran. We go walking in the hills or else for excursions down the river, fishing (with earthworms) after O'Hallaran discovered a couple of old rods in the garage and gave them a rub-down. I recognised one of the rods, having used it a quarter of a century ago as an adolescent fly fisher. For a week, every morning, we collect bait from the compost heap at the edge of the vegetable garden and make our way down to the bend in the stream at the bottom of Morgan's field. O'Hallaran insists on showing me how to thread the wriggling worms onto the hook and while we fish, we chat, and he tells me about his life as a vagabond.

He tells me that during his travels he would sometimes find work as a gardener, his preferred occupation, and this necessitated travelling with some essential tools, which were occasionally confiscated by over-zealous customs officers, or policemen, who considered the tools of his trade as potentially lethal weapons. These he would replace on an *ad hoc* basis. He once worked as a gardener, he tells me, at a castle near Bratislava that had belonged to the Countess Elizabeth Báthory who, in the sixteenth century, was accused of the murder of six hundred and fifty virgins, in whose blood she liked to bathe. The Countess was found guilty, but because of her aristocratic status (she was cousin to the Prince of Transylvania) could not be sentenced to death, and was instead confined to one of her castles, under house arrest, as it were, although accompanied by a staff of many servants. The castle chosen was the one near Bratislava, where O'Hallaran worked as a gardener. He said he had seen the Countess – or her ghost – one evening, standing on the battlements, after the tourists had left, that it could only have been her, could only have been the Countess Báthory, he was certain of it, staring out over the wide Danube. There she stood, claimed O'Hallaran, majestic on the ramparts, oblivious to the passage of centuries, her cheeks flushed with fresh virginal blood, as she howled for her own lost youth.

He could spin a yarn, could O'Hallaran, with his full head of hair, his rosy cheeks, his red nose and his bullshit. To the outsider, at least, our situation might have appeared quite cosy: two male friends, who go out fishing of a morning and exchange travellers' tales; two lifelong female friends; and linking the various pairings of this quartet and forming, at least to my mind, the most meaningful bond, were myself and Alice, represented (as I imagined at times) by the king and queen carved into the fireplace at the heart of Llys Rhosyn.

My last visit to the blue tent began to recede in significance and perhaps I was negligent, certainly I missed the warning signs (but we shall come to that), perhaps I even came to enjoy the relative stability of the new domestic arrangement

– but the tent, I discovered, had not forgotten my most recent visit, and nor did it withhold from me for much longer what I had, in my ignorance, called forth from it.

The newcomer's presence was announced to us without anything ever being seen; by absence. More specifically, by the disappearance of food from the kitchen table and then later, from the refrigerator. I have no idea how long the visitor had been in residence. Perhaps, like Gabrielle and O'Hallaran, the visitor came among us immediately after I left the tent on the last occasion, when I was awakened by O'Hallaran in the middle of my bad red dream, as I began to think of it. The bad red dream stood out against the others; the good blue dream that presaged the arrival of Alice, the rustic green dream that heralded O'Hallaran, and the yellow or golden dream that presaged the coming of Gabrielle. But I am confusing myself with all this talk of colours; I do not even know if these were the true colours of the dreams or visions, or whether I have attributed them in hindsight. But of all the visits I paid to the blue tent, the fourth was the most dramatic and upsetting, and it affected me more powerfully than all of the other visits combined.

I'm not sure if I was the first to notice food disappearing, but I was the first to follow it up. It was a balmy evening, and we were eating outside. And it was not the fox that stole the food this time. The fox would not have run away, not when there was more food available on the other plates; he would have hung around for second helpings. I was clearing the table, after our meal. The others had gone in. I had taken most of the plates inside, and the cutlery, but I had left my own plate outside, because I was not hungry that evening, and had left most of the meal, a pasta dish that Gabrielle had cooked. Delicious, or it would normally have been delicious, I am sure, but I had no appetite. I also left the salt and pepper on the table. That was how I noticed. I returned from the kitchen

154

to pick up the last remaining plate, my own, and the pepper pot and salt cellar. In fact, I was intending to transfer my uneaten pasta onto an old tin dish, on which we left food for the fox, but when I returned from the kitchen to retrieve it, the food was gone. Our visitor hadn't even waited for me to put the food in the fox's bowl. They had run off with my half-portion of pasta, and the salt cellar.

There was a faint breeze moving the leaves, and dusk was darkening the woods. I felt I was being watched, precisely as I had the first time I emerged from the tent, when I set off up the trail through the woods, and looked down and saw Alice (who I did not know was Alice) walking down the drive, a bouquet of wild flowers in her hand. That feeling that you are somehow prey, or else the subject of another's gaze. I looked up at the woods but could see nothing. The crows were quiet. I don't know about the buzzard. I hadn't seen the buzzard for a month or so. I hadn't seen the buzzard since that day when I watched it being attacked by crows, while sitting at my desk in the library, looking out through the big latticed window.

And then, when I realised the pasta was missing, and the salt, I thought back, and realised that Alice had mentioned only the day before about leaving some toast on her plate at breakfast, turning her back to put more coffee on, and when she returned to her place, the toast being gone. It was a sunny morning, and the back door was open. Yes, the back door was open and her toast went missing. Someone might have snuck in quickly, grabbed the toast and run off through the open door. Someone with hands, rather than paws. Someone who was watching from outside, while hidden, from behind the half-open door, or peering through the crack between the hinges, waiting for their moment.

Someone was stealing our food. Someone was stealing our salt. And it was not the fox.

29

I look around carefully. The crows, as I have mentioned, are silent, and the songs of the other birds are muted, an unusual state of affairs on an early summer's evening. I, of course, with the ridiculous sensitivity to such things brought on by my maddening insomnia, immediately begin to read *meaning* into this, but it frequently happens that there is a lull in birdsong on a June evening. This is a fact.

I wonder where the thief could have gone. I have heard nothing – although of course I was inside the kitchen when the theft took place, and O'Hallaran and Alice are washing and drying the dishes, that is the arrangement because Gabrielle has done the cooking, and she is curled up in the single armchair in the kitchen, reading a sports magazine. So I hear nothing, only the background buzz of their conversation as Alice and O'Hallaran stand by the sink, chatting as they always do. And I don't say anything to the others about the disappeared food at this point, instead returning outside on my own, feeling slightly exhilarated by the mystery.

For a few moments I enjoy standing there on the patio outside the library, listening to the absence of birdsong. I wonder about the fox. I half expect to see him standing at the edge of the woods, his snout quivering in the air and tail erect, trying to discern if there is any supper for him tonight. But perhaps the fox knows better. Perhaps Foxy knows he has a competitor and is not going to show. Animals know these things.

I begin to pace towards the vegetable garden. If the thief has been watching me clear the table, then he (or she, or it) will have had to calculate how much time they need to steal the food and hurry back to safety before I return outside to collect the remaining items and potentially catch them in the act. They will have chosen the quickest route back to the nearest hiding place, and that would mean sprinting to the vegetable garden where the runner beans have grown tall, or the greenhouse, where the tomato and ganja plants provide ample cover. So there I go, taking my time, and I search for any traces, any tracks on the ground, but can find none, or else am not observant enough to spot any. I stand in the greenhouse, inhaling the rich perfume of tomatoes and *cannabis sativa*, before stepping outside and wondering where to search next.

The path in front of me leads directly up to the woodshed, where O'Hallaran hid after being ousted from the tent. It seems an unlikely hiding place for someone who needs to be on the constant look-out, but what do I know? I follow the track towards the shed.

My first impression, on stepping inside, even with the door ajar, is the darkness of the place. It is hard to make things out. I push the door shut behind me. My eyes take a while to become accustomed to the dark, but I notice a thin shaft of light, a narrow luminous beam filled with motes of dust that traverses the shed in a straight line from the door, and turning back I see a bright aperture in the door itself. A hole has been bored into the wood, a spy-hole, an inch in diameter, and I am sure it was not there before, when I visited the shed with Alice, following Gabrielle's assault on O'Hallaran. Someone must has drilled this hole very recently, but with what?

I pick up one of the heavier logs and wedge it against the door, forcing it wide open, to ensure the greatest possible amount of light comes in. This gives me a better overview. On one side, to my right, stands the old-fashioned lawn-mower, a petrol-run machine, which once, last autumn, I had attempted to start, but gave up and called in a proper gardener, or so-called landscaper, who used his own buggy-type mower and spent an entire day around the grounds, charging me so much I never asked him back. There are also shovels, rakes, two wheelbarrows, an assortment of buckets, a few items whose purpose I do not recognise, and some sheets of tarpaulin. Lying on top of the tarpaulin is an old-fashioned hand drill, a so-called brace and bit, clearly the tool used to make a spy-hole in the door. A few shavings of wood around the base of the door frame complete the evidence. The shed is large, by the standard of sheds, and the supply of logs seemingly inexhaustible. Rows of them stretch back towards the end of the structure. And then I notice, towards the left-hand side, a gap in the stack of wood, where a section has been removed and the missing logs lie scattered nearby. This opening is too small to accommodate an adult.

Lowering myself onto my haunches, I examine the space, which forms the opening of a tunnel. The distance to the wall is six feet at most, and at the end of the tunnel, staring at me with big eyes, barefoot and shivering, is a child.

When I say a child – although it takes me a few seconds to discern this in the dusk – I mean a boy: at least, this is my first impression. He has long dirty hair, light brown in colour and falling over the eyes, although parting naturally in the centre. Then I am not so certain, and my first impression is immediately superseded by a second, that the child is a girl. Boy or girl, it hardly matters. A child is living in the shed; filthy, undernourished, unshod, its face smeared with snot and gunge. It is wrapped in a blanket that I recognise as having disappeared a week or so back after Gabrielle and Alice had been sunbathing on the back lawn. And held tight in its right hand, clutching it like a crucifix against impending evil, is the salt cellar.

It takes me a while to adjust to this scene. The kid keeps staring at me. I guess I am supposed to make some kind of first move, to speak to it. I am not very good with children. I mean, I am not very good with adults, but am significantly worse with children. I am not even sure how old it could be. Six perhaps? Seven? I have not really had any cause to take notice of the age of children since I ceased being a child myself. Apart from my visits to Llys Rhosyn and Aunt Megan, my childhood, as I must have intimated (and if I haven't, I should have), was not a happy one and I have found no need to revisit it by proxy, as it were, by associating regularly with children. I decide to speak to it then, as though I were speaking to an adult.

What are you doing here, in the woodshed? I say, in a friendly fashion. And I feel like an idiot, because already I know for a fact that the child will not answer. Instead, without taking its eyes off me, it carefully shakes some salt from the cellar into the open palm of its left hand, and licks it, licks the left palm clean. Licks it two or three times, and then, although there cannot be any more salt left, continues licking its own palm, and in between these slow brushes of the tongue, looks up at me, as if sending me a message of some kind. This disturbs me. I want it to desist, but do not know how to make it stop. I do not know how to make it do anything without frightening it. So I ask it a question.

What is your name?

It stares at me with renewed intensity, its eyes bulging. The eyes have long dark lashes, darker than the hair on its head.

It starts to dribble. I am even more upset than when it started licking itself. It doesn't seem to be aware that it is dribbling, the thin stream of bubbly saliva hanging from its lower lip. Then it lifts its free hand and wipes its mouth. I am relieved. I am glad that this has happened. It means that

159

the child, the boy or girl, has the ability to stem the tide of dribble, to clean itself, to look after itself, if only in a rudimentary way. This gesture – along with the evident ability to operate a brace and bit – suggests that the child is not an imbecile.

I crook my finger and make a beckoning gesture. Will the child recognise this signal? Apparently not. It looks at me with profound distrust, imbued with an element of sadness, and shakes its head, once, twice, raising the chin slightly, in a strange, affecting movement. It is a gesture which, inexplicably, causes a flickering of loss and grief to settle in my stomach, and my eyes brim with tears, which I brush away with my sleeve at once, unconsciously mimicking the action of the child wiping away its dribble. The child's head-shaking suggests that there is nothing that I can do, that my tears – if it is responding to my tears – are of no use. In this gesture I recognise hopelessness on an epic scale.

I am at a loss how to act. I cannot crawl along the little passageway that the child has constructed (skilfully, I must concede) by taking apart a large section of logs and re-arranging them to form a tunnel, as I am too large, or the tunnel too small. My only chance might be to coax the child out, but I have nothing with which to tempt it.

I must stop reacting emotionally, and start thinking. Evidently the child has a passion for salt. This in itself is quite odd. I would normally expect a child to be tempted by sweet things. But to date, if the disappearances are any indication, the child has shown a preference for savoury food, including salted crisps and olives. And it enjoys licking salt from the palm of its hand. Then I remember that there is some cold bacon in the fridge: O'Hallaran cooked a fry-up for breakfast that morning, and there was some leftover bacon. I could go back down to the house and fetch the bacon. I would then attempt to lure the waif from its hiding place with a tasty morsel of pig-meat.

Listen, I say (although I have no way of knowing whether the child understands a word I am saying), I am going down to the house for something. I won't be a minute. You stay here, right? Don't go running off anywhere.

It continues to stare at me with lustrous eyes.

My fear is that once I leave the shed, the child will dart out behind me and run off into the woods. I cannot risk this. I need some help. So I leave the shed, take a few paces down the hill towards the house, and I shout for Alice. I can hear the strains of panic in my own voice and it must sound as if something terrible has happened, but this does not matter if it has the desired effect. Which it does, eventually, when she appears in the doorway of the house. I have a flashback to that first time I watched Alice open the back door, when I was looking down on the house from the fallen trunk at the top of the woods, and realise that now, like then, she is wearing blue jeans and a black top.

What's going on? she shouts back at me. What's happened? Have you had an accident?

Come up here, I yell back. I need your help.

When Alice reaches me, I have walked a few more paces down the hill towards her.

There's a child, I say, breathlessly, hiding in the woodshed. I'm worried that it might try to run off. I think it needs help, but I can't reach it.

Can't reach it?

You'll see. It's made itself a little nest. It likes salt. It likes salty food. I thought I'd go down to the kitchen to fetch some bacon, as bait, to lure it out, but I didn't want to leave it alone in the shed in case it runs off into the woods and we can't find it and it dies of malnutrition or exposure. So I want you to keep an eye on the kid, talk to it, don't let it get frightened, while I go down to get some food. It's hungry. It's been taking food from us. It's where the missing food's been going. Just go inside, you'll see what to do.

It? Girl or boy?

I have no idea. You decide.

And so I return to the shed with Alice, open the door, and show her where the child is hiding, still squatting at the end of its little tunnel.

Then I run back down to the house.

I don't see O'Hallaran or Gabrielle in the kitchen. I am in a hurry, as the incident with the strange child is, I am sure, the delayed product of the tent, and I am obsessed with all that the tent brings me. Obsessed, and now disturbed. I had thought that perhaps the tent had come to the end of its projections or ejaculations, but apparently it was saving its biggest surprise until last. I rummage in the fridge, find the few cooked rashers that O'Hallaran has left there for his pal, the fox, and return up the hill to the shed.

The door of the woodshed remains jammed open, so I have a clear view inside as I step over the threshold. Alice is sitting with her back to the wall, in much the same place as O'Hallaran occupied when I found him on the night that everything happened. She is sitting there, and nestled into her side, its head nuzzling against her neck, its thin legs wrapped around her waist, is the child. It makes no sound, but clings to her like a frightened monkey.

Well, I say, you've made progress. I step towards Alice and the child raises its head, fixing me with its big eyes, still nervous of me, but no longer quite so fearful, now that it has found its protector.

How did you get it to come out? Has it spoken yet? I say. Alice doesn't answer at first.

162

The poor child is traumatised, she says, eventually. By not attaching any gender to the utterance, I take it that she is as confused about its gender as I am.

I wave the rashers of bacon in the air, and take a step closer towards them. Alice takes one from me, and when she offers the strip of meat to the child, a small hand emerges and takes it, slowly, tentatively, but then, with extraordinary speed, delivers it to its mouth, and it bolts the food, barely chewing, like a dog. It holds out its hand for another rasher. I pass them on to Alice.

They sit there against the wall, Alice feeding bacon to the foundling child. I am utterly external to the scenario, apart from serving as a bacon-dispenser. I can offer nothing more. The picture in front of me reminds me of some primitive rendition of Madonna and child. In which case, I conclude, I am the painter.

30

Alice carries the child back down to the house, still wrapped in its blanket. She, like the child, does not seem to need any help from me.

We had better give it a bath, I suggest.

Alice does not respond.

How did you get it out from its hiding place? I ask.

She sighs, heavily. I sat at the opening of the tunnel, she says, and it ran into my arms. And that is all she says, as if, by omission, she implies other things.

In the kitchen we are greeted by Gabrielle. The child studies her carefully, but makes no response when Gabrielle speaks to it, cooingly, in French. Alice asks Gabrielle to go and run a bath for the child. I am offended that she seems to be ignoring me, when it was I who brought the child's presence to her attention. How come Alice has so effortlessly taken command of the situation? Whose house is this anyway?

I stand around, feeling useless. I wish O'Hallaran were here, so that we could feel useless together.

I decide to make some coffee, by way of appearing occupied. When the electric mill starts making its grinding noises, the child is startled and looks up, but does not cry out, or weep. In fact, it has not cried since I discovered it. Unlike me. I am the only one who has wept. The child has merely observed us in turn, either anxiously, as at first it watched me, or in a state of fear, or – as now, from a position of safety, secure in Alice's arms – with raw curiosity. Alice holds it lightly, but close against her body. If the child really is six or seven, as I first guessed, it is small for its age.

I am upset that my few comments have been disregarded by Alice, and I do not want to face her disdainful or accusing gaze. I pour myself an espresso, and when I turn around I see that Alice has left the kitchen, along with the child. She has left without speaking, presumably to join Gabrielle in the bathroom. So I drink my coffee alone, and I stare out of the kitchen window, at the blue tent. I see O'Hallaran, standing to one side of the tent, in the failing light. He is sharpening a long stick, a kind of stake – the sort traditionally used for skewering vampires – with a large knife. He is lost in concentration and does not notice me, watching him from the window. I realise, once again, how tired I am. I am so very, very tired. My eyes are sore and my eyelids are heavy.

I settle into the kitchen armchair, which is covered with faded Regency stripes, in soft, satiny material. I curl into the chair, drain my coffee, and fall asleep. I immediately begin to dream that I am in a Turkish or Levantine bazaar, perhaps Istanbul or Beirut, and I am lost in the endless alleyways of the market, one I almost certainly visited in my travels, I forget the name, of course I forget the name, why must I always forget the names of things, of places, of a market known to me, even one that is profoundly familiar from the time I lived in Istanbul, I assume it is Istanbul, it may be Beirut or Izmir or even Alexandria or Damascus or ancient Tarsus for all I know, where tradesmen are calling out, yelling the names of their wares, some of them occasionally following me down the aisles and shouting words at me that I cannot understand, in a language I have never learned, or have partially learned but cannot now recall. One of them produces a child, a scrawny urchin, and presents him to me. Over the salesman's free arm, a carpet is draped. You buy my carpet, he says, I throw in the child. I recognise the salesman. I met him once before, in a dream or in fact, outside the Blue

Mosque in Sultanahmet. Only ten thousand lira for the carpet, he says, and the child for free. I look at the child and I recognise him too, I have known him always, but cannot remember from where. I feel a burgeoning sadness, and know that again I am tearful. When I wake, I am rubbing away the tears. I am not alone.

I cannot have slept for long, but it was long enough for Alice to have bathed the foundling. She stands before me, the child held upright at her hip, Gabrielle at her side. Alice, who appears to have bathed also (her hair is wet and she has changed into a patterned cotton dress) seems in her element, as though made for this display of surrogate motherhood. The snot stains and grunge have vanished from the child's face. Instead it looks scrubbed and shiny, although its expression could not be described as cheerful. It is, if anything, intensely thoughtful, with that fixed studiousness at which the very young are so expert. Its skin is of a natural light olive complexion, which was difficult to discern before. The women have dressed it in clean shorts, a T-shirt and jumper, which I recognise as Alice's, and all of them far too big, the shorts coming down to its shins. So the child is dressed, if still barefoot. Its feet have been washed, however: they are no longer encrusted with dirt as they were when I first found it.

We tried out some socks, says Alice, but you would have thought we were carrying out some terrible torture, what with all the screaming and shouting. Nice soft cosy socks they were too, she says, admonishing the kid in a child-friendly voice. So we stayed barefoot.

We? Alice has turned into Mary Poppins.

And then I recognise something else in the child, now that layers of grime have been removed from its face: it reminds me of myself, or rather of the way I appeared in photographs when I was a child. The realisation stabs at me. I stare at the kid long and hard. It is more than a mere resemblance. There can be no doubt about it: I am looking at an image of myself aged six, the year my mother died.

I do not get up from the armchair, but remain seated, the three of them lined up before me. I can tell that Alice's attitude towards me has mellowed. But why was she hostile before? When we brought the child down from the shed to the kitchen, what could she have been thinking? That I had hurt it in some way? Could she really consider me capable of such a thing? That Alice might think I had harmed the kid makes me weak with incomprehension.

Just then O'Hallaran enters the kitchen through the back door, whistling. He stops short at the scene before him.

What have we here? he says, putting on a face that certain adults reserve for interactions with small children and animals, and he approaches the child, raising his hand as if to chuck it under the chin. The child immediately flinches and buries its face in the crook of Alice's neck.

Well, if that's the way it's going to be … says O'Hallaran, shaking his head. And he makes his way over to the coffee machine, unconcerned.

Anyone else for a cup? he asks, looking over in my direction. Not for me, I say, but make yourself at home.

Meanwhile, Gabrielle, at Alice's side, has adopted the role of assistant nanny, or rather nanny to Alice's mummy. I need to speak to one of the women. I get up from the chair and, so as not to upset the child by demanding Alice's attention, I take Gabrielle by the arm, leading her through the door that connects with the living room. The mere act of touching her, of leading her physically from the room, feeling the silk of her blouse under my fingers, makes me dizzy. I catch the scent of her shampoo, spring flowers.

167

Well? I ask, steeling myself against the wave of desire that has swept over me: Did you make any discoveries? Did you manage to get it to speak? I'm sorry, I am still calling it *it*. If you gave it a bath you must know by now whether it's a boy or a girl.

Gabrielle looks flustered for a moment, and actually blushes.

It is neither, she says, and hesitates – or rather, both. It is, how would you call it … *ambiguous?*

You mean intersex? I say, helping her out.

You don't say *hermaphrodite?*

I don't think so, not nowadays. It's inaccurate, and probably demeaning.

Gabrielle nods, thoughtfully, and smiles. Then, lowering her voice, she tells me there were no signs of harm to the child, no bruising or indications of maltreatment. A few scratches, that could have been the result of wandering barefoot through the woods, nothing more. The child, she tells me … is *feral*. I am so relieved, about it not being injured, I say – I would be sick to know that someone had hurt the child.

And before I know it, I am overcome by a fresh attack of tearfulness, and Gabrielle takes my hands and holds them between her own. She turns and brushes a loose strand of hair behind my ear – my hair has grown long, it is months since I had it cut.

Don't worry, she says. We'll look after the child. And then, more softly, as she brushes my cheek with the backs of her fingers: *we'll take care of you.*

And this time she does turn back into the kitchen, to re-join Alice and the waif.

I choose to ignore her final remark, about *taking care of me*. But how, I wonder, does she propose that we – whoever 'we' are – take care of the child? Not, I imagine, by reporting its appearance to the police, or by calling Social Services and passing the child into their care. So, what? By illegally adopting it into our little household, with its ready-made quartet of weirdo mammies and pappies?

Rather than follow Gabrielle to the kitchen, I retire to the library, distracted both by Gabrielle, and by my recognition of the child as being a replica of – or identical to – my own younger self. At the rear of the library is a small store room, where I have rummaged on many occasions, and in which Megan kept several boxes of photographs. Among them should be one that will settle the matter of the child's looks, if not its identity. When I reach the storeroom, however, I find that someone has been there before me. I knew from earlier visits to the room that it contained boxes of old things, other than photos: souvenirs from Megan's travels; exotica from India and the Far East; brightly-coloured miniature paintings that I recognised from the street-sellers of Central America; trinkets; caskets of jewellery; fragments of pottery; coloured stones and buttons. But there was something wrong about their careless arrangement – Megan was always scrupulous about packing things away in neatly ordered piles – and the boxes look as if they have been searched and plundered, their contents removed and hurriedly re-arranged.

When I return to the kitchen, Keto the hound has joined the little menagerie. Alice is now in the chair, the child on her lap, the dog at her feet. I think how naturally the dog has become a part of things at Llys Rhosyn – no, how easily he attached himself to Alice; how he seemed to need little or no training, especially when I consider what Morgan told me about the dog's unruliness, how he was untrainable. Perhaps Keto was looking for Alice all along, when he came and stood outside the house the day of her arrival, and then launched himself at the car the following day. And from some distant memory I recall the legend that a ghost dog will precede the appearance of its owner.

I look around the room. How busy things have become in my kitchen! My little empire is thriving, has borne issue. I again think of the Madonna and child in a particularly dark and vegetable rendition.

Have you tried speaking to it in other languages? I ask.

Her, says Alice. We cannot keep calling her *it*. Woman, as you know, is the first gender; the template. And she allows herself a smile.

So, I say, returning to my question. French, of course. Anything else?

Italian, says Gabrielle, when we were upstairs.

Spanish, says Alice. No reaction to these.

I could try some Turkish, says O'Hallaran, who is leaning against the sink, his back to the window. A little Slovakian perhaps.

And he moves across the room, kneels down in front of the child, and utters a soft torrent of a language I recognise as Turkish. The kid, safe from her perch on Alice's knee now regards O'Hallaran with a sort of detached but vague interest, as though he were a courtier returning from the colonies with a rare orchid. There is no indication that the child recognises any of the words that O'Hallaran is uttering, whether in Turkish, or in the language that follows. I have my doubts about O'Hallaran's Slovakian, but I let it pass. It could equally have been Czech or Polish for all I knew, or none of these: a concoction of O'Hallaran's. His performance, while having a negligible effect on the child, amuses Gabrielle, who rolls her eyes and grins at me.

Heavens, I think, we are a polyglot bunch. But we haven't

tried Welsh yet, which, after all, might have been the best place to start, before embarking on the likes of Slovakian.

So I try Welsh. I attempt a couple of lines of a nursery rhyme, and to my amazement – to the amazement of all of us – the child begins to laugh.

Yes, he (I adhere to this gender, obviously) laughs out loud; a raw, keening sound, showing his teeth, and then breaks off into a staccato giggle before coming to a stop, and returning to silence, turning back towards Alice and resting his head on her breast, but – and this is encouraging – keeping one eye on me.

What did you say? says Alice, excited. What were the words of the song?

I say them this time, not singing:

Dau gi bach yn mynd i'r coed
Esgyd newydd ar bob troed
dau gi bach yn dwad adre
wedi colli un o'u sgidiau

This time the child does not react with mirth, nor even with a smile, but still keeps his eyes fixedly on me. So it was the singing he responded to, perhaps, rather than the language.

In English? asks Gabrielle.

Two little dogs go to the woods, new shoes on their feet. Two little dogs come back home, missing one shoe each.

Or they never come back, I think.

Peace they say, to the dog whose life is short.

I thought it seemed an appropriate choice, I say, seeing as the kid has no shoes.

I am quite pleased with myself, getting the only joyful reaction so far from the child, after being treated like a paedophile by Alice at the start of this episode. It also amuses me that my friends, my house guests, call them what you will, should have gone through their expansive repertoire of languages before any of them thought of the language of this country, of my childhood and my ancestors, as well – more significantly – as the first language of Megan, whose spirit so evidently pervades the house and unites the four of us adults in our dealings with each other and with her legacy.

But in spite of all efforts I make to get the child to respond in some way to further renditions of my rusty Welsh, either spoken or sung, I draw a blank. I start to think that the kid was laughing at me, rather than at the words of the song, or in recognition of the language. At best my singing might have stirred a memory, but nothing more. Instead, he scratches his nose, sneezes a few times, even strokes the dog, nervously at first, and then with more enthusiasm, before abruptly losing interest, and remaining resolutely silent.

Carla, says Alice, for no reason that I can figure: let's call her Carla.

Or Carlo, I mutter, half under my breath.

We could kind of mumble the last syllable, suggests O'Hallaran.

This is so stupid, says Gabrielle. *La Pauvre petite.* I mean, why should we care whether Carla, or Carlo, is a boy or a girl?

We may not mind, I continue, but out there, in the big bad world, people are expected to fit in with out-dated gender categories, and are judged if they do not. For instance, children have to know which lavatories to use at school. Otherwise life can become hell for them.

So she would be better off here with us then, says Alice. She is inspired, on a mission. She says again: Carla would be better staying here with us. Here at Llys Rhosyn. No possible harm can come to us here, all safe together. And she hugs the child, who, if I am not mistaken, looks rather worried at her carer's sudden change of mood, from one of motherly concern to protective zeal.

Wouldn't we be breaking the law? I venture. Wouldn't it be safe to assume that the child belongs to somebody? That he, or she, has parents?

Why would you assume that? says Alice. What makes you think this is a human child?

31

From this point on, I need to act for myself, to stop the others from taking over my life … or attempting to steal from me. My bedroom, the library storeroom; where else have they been searching? And, of course, if I had been vigilant from the start, if I had been just a little more observant, and less fixated on the tent, I would have recognised that this has been going on all along. But because none of the characters in my story were in an outright manner dangerous or malicious, because I trusted them, befriended them, was attracted to and even (probably, possibly, perhaps) slept with at least one of them, it does not occur to me that Llys Rhosyn has become a house of thieves, a place of shadows …

It is only a matter of time before the child falls asleep in Alice's arms. Since it is approaching midnight, it is decided – the women decide – that rather than put her to bed on the sofa in the living room, or in one of the spare rooms, where she (I may as well go along with this) might wake up alone and afraid, Carla will sleep with Alice and Gabrielle in their large double bed. I agree to this, as it suits my emerging plan. Keep them together. O'Hallaran bids us all goodnight and sets off, I assume, for the tent, while I explain to Alice that I need to speak with her, alone, in the library. Alice nods, quite solemnly, and hands the sleeping child to Gabrielle, who ascends the stairs to their bedroom.

In the library I sit at my desk, in the red leather chair. Alice seats herself directly in front of me on the desk itself, swinging her legs.

First things first. I show her the photograph I found in the storeroom – of myself as a young child.

Alice exclaims out loud, as though in surprise. Then she smiles, without displaying any confusion; frankly, as though far too easily relieved of her initial display of amazement; as though surprise were the response that I required rather than one that she genuinely experienced.

Do you not find it strange, I ask, that the child who appeared in the woodshed is, or would once have been, to all appearances, my double?

Alice shrugs, and looks away.

And why would she find it strange? This is the woman who not so long ago uttered the words: *What makes you think this is a human child?*

I know what you're all looking for, I say to her, after a while. Ever since O'Hallaran told me his story about finding something in the maize field, the silver cylinder that he gave to Megan in exchange for the tent. Is that why he came here? Is that why you came?

Wearily, she says: O'Hallaran isn't anyone, you know.

What do you mean by that? I ask.

Well, she says – and I anticipate another demonstration of her alarming logic – it is quite clear to me, at least, that O'Hallaran is not who he says he is. Why then should he be anyone at all?

But that doesn't make sense, I say: everyone has an identity, a personal history.

Alice remains silent.

After a while she says: No, everyone doesn't, don't you see?

Why, I ask, did O'Hallaran tell me the story of the Aleph? It was virtually the first thing he told me. Why would he alert me to the fact that he knew of its existence? He needn't have.

I've no idea, Alice replies. You're the one in charge.

And then: Is that what it's called? An Aleph?

She returns to swinging her legs beneath the table, and

begins to whistle a sad tune, her eyes raised dreamily to the wooden beams that straddle the library ceiling.

As I watch Alice, I have a sense that she is less tangible, less real to me, than at any time since arriving at my house. She is drifting away. In order to reassure myself, I lean forward and touch her cheek with my hand, just as Gabrielle had touched mine, before telling me that they (she and Alice) would 'look after me'. I wonder just how they envisaged doing that.

Alice is pliant, unresisting. There is an absence about her, which I cannot explain away by her apparent indifference to the evidence provided by the photograph, by her inability to answer my questions. Something is diminishing in her; her substantiality is breaking down. She is fragmenting, becoming less solid.

She slumps forward, but I catch her before she falls, lift her from the desk and carry her across the library to the fireplace. She is almost weightless, her arms around my neck. I settle her gently in Megan's green armchair.

I know that I have to return her, return all of them to the place from which they have come; the other world from which the tent has disgorged them; the other world that the Aleph has made visible to me.

Aleph. The first letter of the Phoenician, Hebrew, Aramaic and Arabic alphabets. The Aleph: a small and miraculous cavity or portal that displays the entire substance of the universe, and all possible worlds.

32

They will drive me insane, I know they will, unless they have already done so. My home has become the haunt of drifting or devious spirits over whom I have no control. I must put them out of the way, these hungry ghosts. I must dream them away, dream them out of existence, back to their own world. To dream, perchance to sleep.

And afterwards, I must write it, somewhere. Yes, I will write it all down, afterwards. Write it, and check it over at my desk in the library, check it through again and again, to make sure the story is recorded exactly as it took place. There at my desk facing the carved fireplace. Otherwise, how can I be sure to remember them in the months and years to come? How else to ensure that the I who tells these things will record them as they happened and will not be swayed by the passing of time into a particular manner of telling things as they are not? The longer I delay, the more likely it is the story will shift its contours and belong to someone else. How do I know I will even be the same person who remembers these things?

I did not say any of this out loud, of course, because if I had, they would not have come with me. There's a difference between thinking things and saying them. If they had known what I knew, if they had read my thoughts, they would never have accompanied me into that night, in the coldest hour, the hour of the wolf, although we have no wolves here, in the Marches, nor in the hinterland, though we had them once, the legend of Gelert vouches for that, and we will have them again, of that I am certain, when our civilisation commits itself to oblivion and all the old savagery returns, but not now, not right now, we have only foxes and the occasional dog, whose life is short.

With this in mind I took Keto the sheepdog to his run and locked him in. I fed him some chopped liver and he settled easily, licking my hand and wagging his tail. I did not want him running around the place, getting under our feet while I carried out my plan.

I started on Alice, of course, otherwise it could not have worked. When I returned to the library I was demanding and insistent, in a way that convinced her that what I was about to do was crucial to the safety of us all. There was no need at all to plead or cajole.

So we went upstairs, Alice and I, and we told Gabrielle of my plan. I had the impression then that she would have done anything for Alice, that she loved her, which was something that I could almost understand, as I had experienced a glimmer of that love myself; but then my feelings have never been clear in that regard. I have always found love to be such a complicated issue. Gabrielle collected the child Carla from the bed. She did not make a sound, wrapped in a shawl, and the two women brought her downstairs, and followed me through the kitchen into the garden; it was a cold night, the stars were visible above the valley, the woods rising like a mantle to the side. I stopped before the tent, unzipped the flap, expecting to be met by the smell of the fox, but the tent was empty, that is to say O'Hallaran was not at home. However, the blanket was still warm, he was not far off, he had wind of us, and I knew what to do, I knew that if we followed my plan he would not be able to stay away, unless of course he had already fled; but why, or how, could he flee without the tent? Where could he possibly go?

So I settled down with Alice to one side of me; she was willing now, because I had won her over before leaving the library; because she trusted me, or because she trusted the tent; because she worshipped Megan and the blue gift my aunt had bestowed on her; or because she was nothing without me, she was whatever I saw, whatever I chose to see at any particular moment, whatever the story, whatever the reason; but I had done with reason, so she lay down beside me anyway; and Gabrielle was willing too, and the child in its shawl, the strange miasma that may or may not have been a human child, who had no choice in the matter, she lay down with us, all four in a row beneath the big blanket we had brought from the double bed in Alice's room, and we waited.

Before daybreak, with the dew rising on the grass outside the tent, I heard him moving outside and then saw his shadow, although even without moonlight he constituted a shadow; I hadn't zipped up the flap, so confident was I that he would return, but I knew he would take his time. In the end he didn't make us wait too long.

I was wondering when you'd come, I said.

Well, he said, it was written from the start.

Was it? It wasn't just my story, it was yours too. Though for a while, as you must have guessed, I didn't know what to believe.

You shouldn't believe anything, he said.

I don't, I said, where you are concerned.

He let that settle for while. No one else made a sound. I had the feeling that Gabrielle was exhausted and wanted to go to sleep, and that Alice was rather sad.

So here we all are, he said, finally, – cosy as hell.

Aren't you going to join us? I asked him, trying to keep it civil.

Do I have any choice? he said.

This matter of choice was still a problem for him, even after telling me the whole thing was a done deal from the outset.

But O'Hallaran knelt, lifted the edge of the blanket, and crawled under. Gabrielle and the child Carla pulled closer to me on my right side. They seemed almost welded together. I drew them towards me and felt them slipping gently inside my body. O'Hallaran took their place beside me. I could feel oblivion begin to swamp me, an opiate sleep infiltrate my senses, a fatigue so profound that I could barely resist it, but I had not finished yet. With my arm around O'Hallaran I pulled him in also, could feel him merge into my right side, slide beneath my ribs. It hurt me, it must have hurt him, but he succumbed. And then, to my left, I sensed Alice closing in, her hair, her fragrance, her warmth, and I turned to kiss her, but she was already dissolving, a vague presence on my left side that settled on my chest and vanished inside me, close to the heart.

Then I slept.

At some point in the night, or the early morning, though I have no memory of it, I must have left the tent, I must have crept back into the house, up the stairs and into my own bed, the bed I so rarely ever sleep in, because it is there that I awaken.

I look at the clock on my bedside table: seven o'clock. It is evening and I have slept through the entire day. But I couldn't care how long I have slept. I care about only one thing. I leap from the bed and hurry to the window.

Drawing aside the curtain I look out onto Morgan's field, and the valley beyond. Of the blue tent there is no sign.

I have the Aleph in my hand, feel its weight, its terrible gravity, so disproportionate to its size; I breathe on its tiny screen, polish it gently with the sleeve of my shirt, and place it on the bedside table, where now it will be safe.

Note:

The poem that appears in Chapter 23 is from the French of Jean Follain, in the author's translation. The original, 'Art de la guerre', was published in *D'après tout*, Paris, Gallimard, 1967.

Parthian Fiction

Hummingbird
Tristan Hughes
ISBN 978-1-91-090190-8
£8.99 ● Paperback

Winner of Edward Standford Award

Winner of Wales Book of the Year People's Choice Award

Pigeon
Alys Conran
ISBN 978-1-91-090123-6
£8.99 ● Paperback

Winner of Wales Book of the Year

Winner of Rhys Davies Award

Ironopolis
Glen James Brown
ISBN 978-1-91-268109-9
£8.99 ● Paperback

'A triumph'
– *The Guardian*

'The most accomplished working-class novel of the last few years.'
– *Morning Star*